Richard Scarry's
Biggest Make-It
Book Ever!

RANDOM HOUSE 🏠 **NEW YORK**

Manufactured in the United States of America   10 9 8 7 6 5 4 3 2 1

How To Use

This Book

You can color these pages with different things . . . crayons, colored pencils, most felt-tip pens, chalks, water colors. The paper is heavy enough to take color on both sides.

The ink of some felt-tip pens will go through to the other side of the page. Make sure you have the right kind of pen! Test your pen by coloring the pencil cup on the opposite page. Did the color go through the paper?

Water colors will make the paper buckle a bit. If you want to keep the paper flat, first tear out your page and tape all 4 sides to heavy cardboard or a drawing board. Masking tape works best. Let your painting dry thoroughly before you take off the tape. On a rainy day, you may have to let your painting dry overnight.

Some pages in this book call for scissors, paste or sticky tape, and other materials besides colors. The directions on these pages will tell you just what you need.

You may find it easier to work on a page if you tear it out first. Here's how to tear without ripping. Fold the page back and forth several times along the perforated line (the line of little punched-out holes). Then hold down the inside margin with one hand and tear gently along the perforated line with the other hand. Out comes the page!

Mr. PAINT PIG

MAKING A CALENDAR

Let's start making a calendar.

There are 12 months in a year. Some months have 30 days and some have 31. February has only 28 days (except in Leap Year, when it has 29). Each calendar page in this book will tell you how many days the month has.

You will want to fill in the numbers for the days of each month. First you must know on which day of the week the month starts. Look at a printed calendar or ask your mother or father to tell you.

Once you know what day a month begins on, write a "1" in the correct square at the top of the calendar page. Then fill in the rest of the numbers for the month. Write the numbers from left to right on each line, just as Huckle has done below.

In some months there may not be enough squares for all the numbers. In that case, the last number or two will have to share a square at the bottom of the calendar. See how Huckle's 31st day is sharing a square?

On Sundays and special holidays you can circle the numbers in red or write them in a different color. Be sure to circle your own birthday!

After you write in all the numbers, color the pictures on the calendar page. Then hang it up in your room.

Now you can start making YOUR calendar. January is on the next page. You will find the rest of the months farther back in the book.

JANUARY						
SUNDAY	MONDAY	TUESDAY	WEDNESDAY	THURSDAY	FRIDAY	SATURDAY
					1	2
③	4	5	6	7	8	9
⑩	11	12	13	14	15	16
⑰	18	19	20	21	22	23
24/31	25	26	27	28	29	30

JANUARY

31 DAYS   NEW YEAR'S DAY—JAN. 1

SUNDAY	MONDAY	TUESDAY	WEDNESDAY	THURSDAY	FRIDAY	SATURDAY

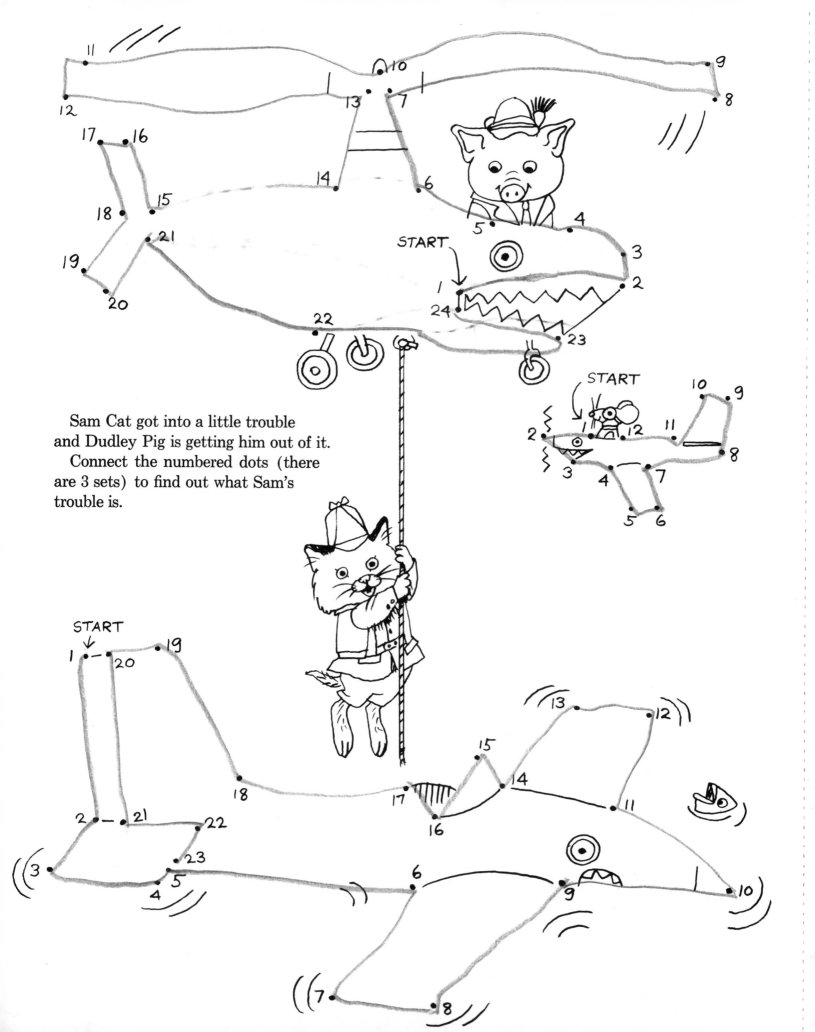

Sam Cat got into a little trouble and Dudley Pig is getting him out of it.
Connect the numbered dots (there are 3 sets) to find out what Sam's trouble is.

Rory and Angus MacWalrus

COLOR MIXING

Kathleen Kitty is going to mix her own colors. Can you mix yours?

Color the worm all over with red, then with yellow—and it will come out orange.

Yellow and blue will give you a green frog.

Now try mixing the colors listed on the other pictures. What do you get?

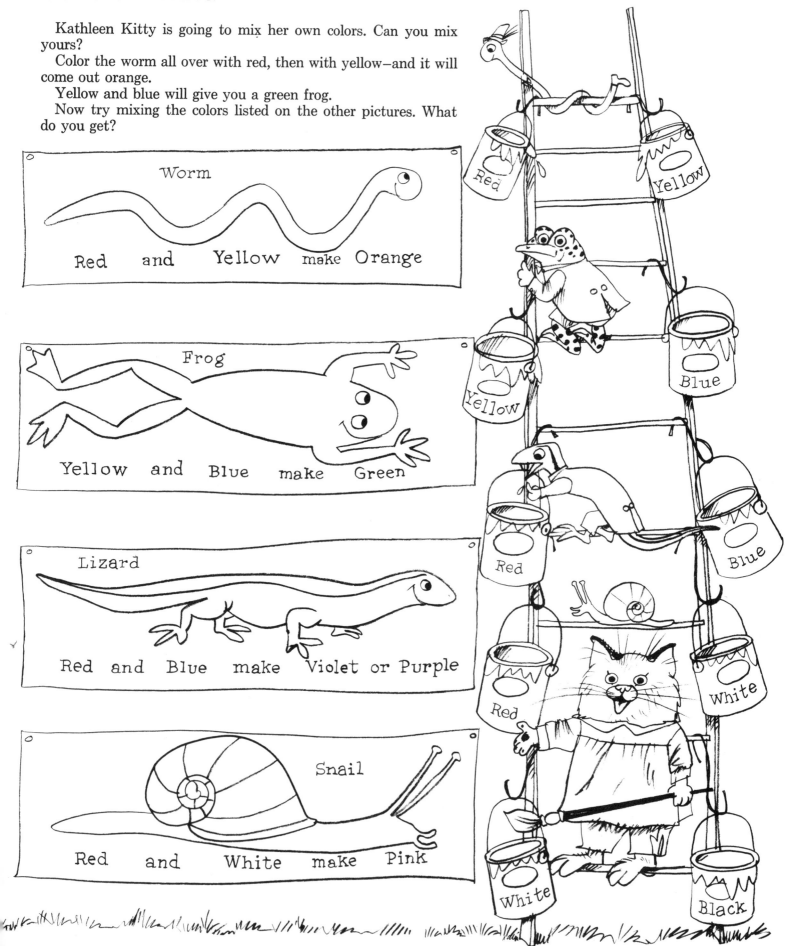

Worm

Red and Yellow make Orange

Frog

Yellow and Blue make Green

Lizard

Red and Blue make Violet or Purple

Snail

Red and White make Pink

THANK-YOU NOTES AND GREETING CARDS

You can use these cards to say "thank you" for presents . . . "get well quick" to a sick friend . . . or to write a short, friendly note. (Have you thanked everyone for your Christmas presents?)

Color the pictures on the cards, front and back. Write your message on the back, on the ruled lines. Cut out the cards, following the outline on this side of the page.

Find the matching envelopes on this page or the next. Card A goes with Envelope A, etc. Directions for making the envelopes are on the next page.

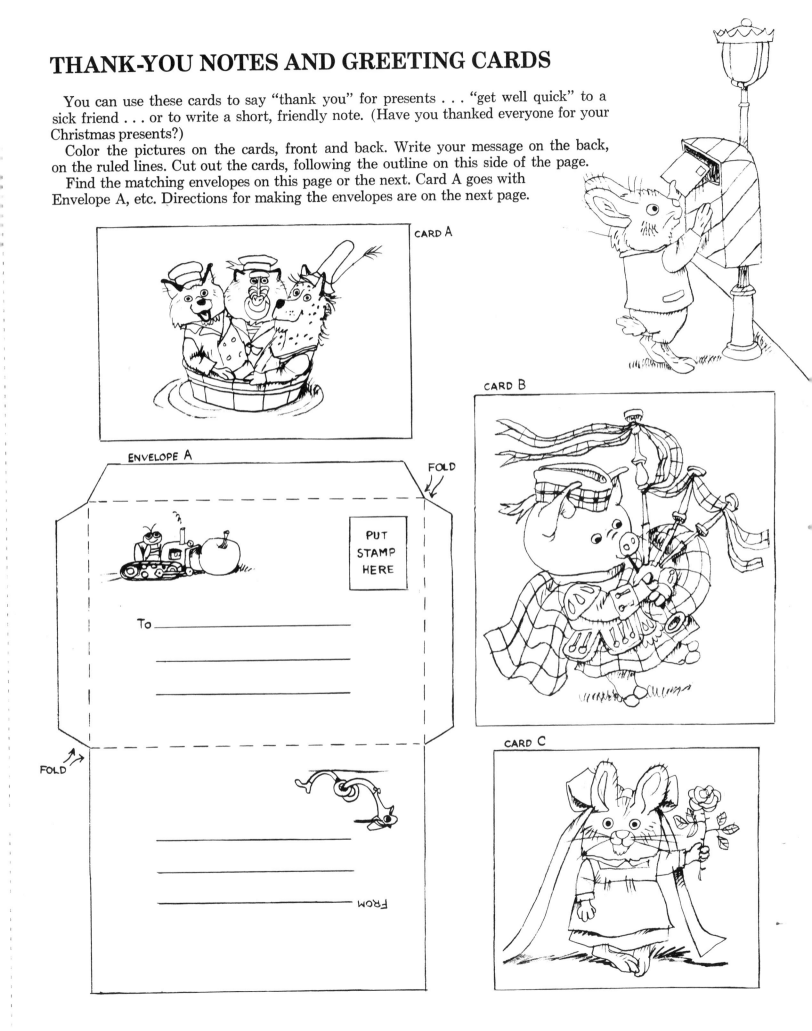

CARD A

CARD B

CARD C

ENVELOPE A

FOLD

PUT
STAMP
HERE

To _____

_____

_____

FOLD

_____

_____

_____

FROM _____

Remember—do your cutting on the other side of the page.

PASTE LAST

PASTE

PASTE

How to make the envelopes for your greeting cards:

Color the pictures on this side of the page. Color the stripes on the other side of the page. Cut each envelope out along the solid black lines. Fold along the dotted lines.

Paste or tape the side tabs to the back of the envelope. Put your card into the envelope, then paste or tape the top tab to the back of the envelope. Address the envelope and put a stamp on it. Then you can mail it.

127,963
127,964

From
Betty Bear
Busytown

BUSYT

To Grandma Bear
West Street
Workville

To Humphfrey Girls
Westport

FOLD

PUT
STAMP
HERE

PUT
STAMP
HERE

To _____

To _____

FOLD

FROM

FROM

ENVELOPE C

ENVELOPE B

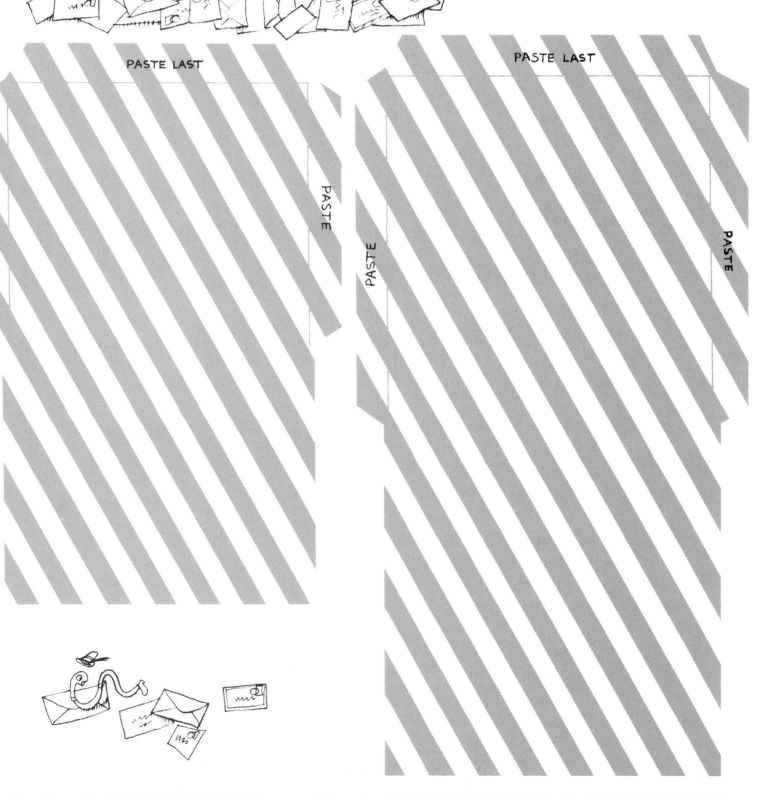

Do your cutting on the other side of the page.

PASTE LAST

PASTE LAST

PASTE

PASTE

PASTE

PASTE

CARS, TRUCKS, AND BUSES

Cars, trucks, and buses are fun to make. Here are 3 pages of them. First color the drawings. Then cut them out along the solid black lines. Fold each car along the dotted lines to make a box. Tuck the side tab inside the box and paste or tape it in place. Then do the same with the roof tab.

PASTE FIRST

PASTE

EXPRESS

EXPRESS

1273

STREET PEOPLE

Color the animals. Then cut them out. Fold the tabs back to make them stand up.

STOP

FOLD

Happy driving!

FOLD

FOLD

PASTE

FOLD

SCHOOL

SCHOOL

SCHOOL

SCHOOL BUS

SCHOOL BUS

SCHOOL

1908

PASTE FIRST

FOLD

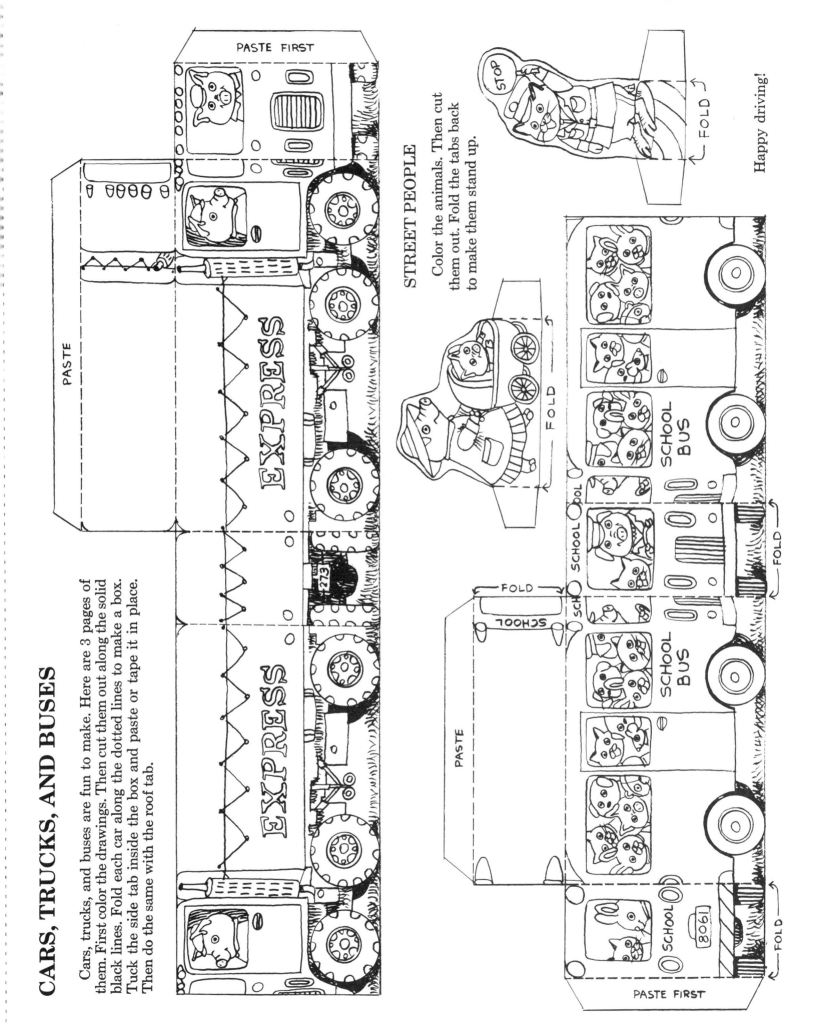

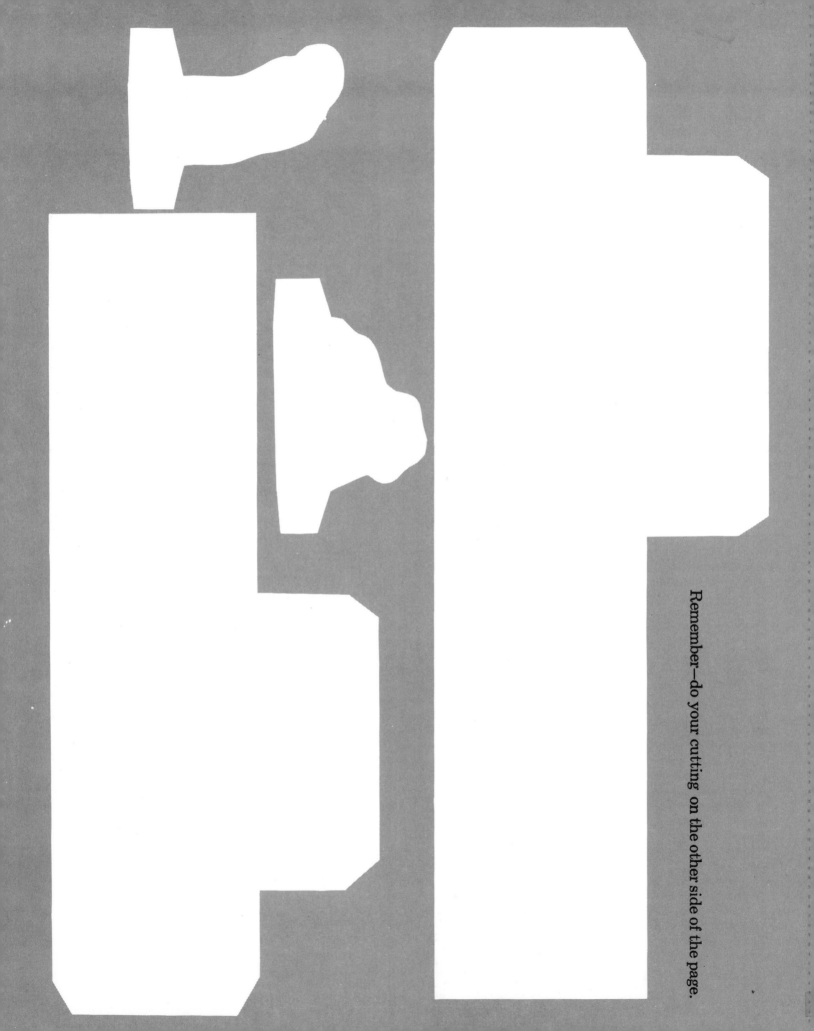

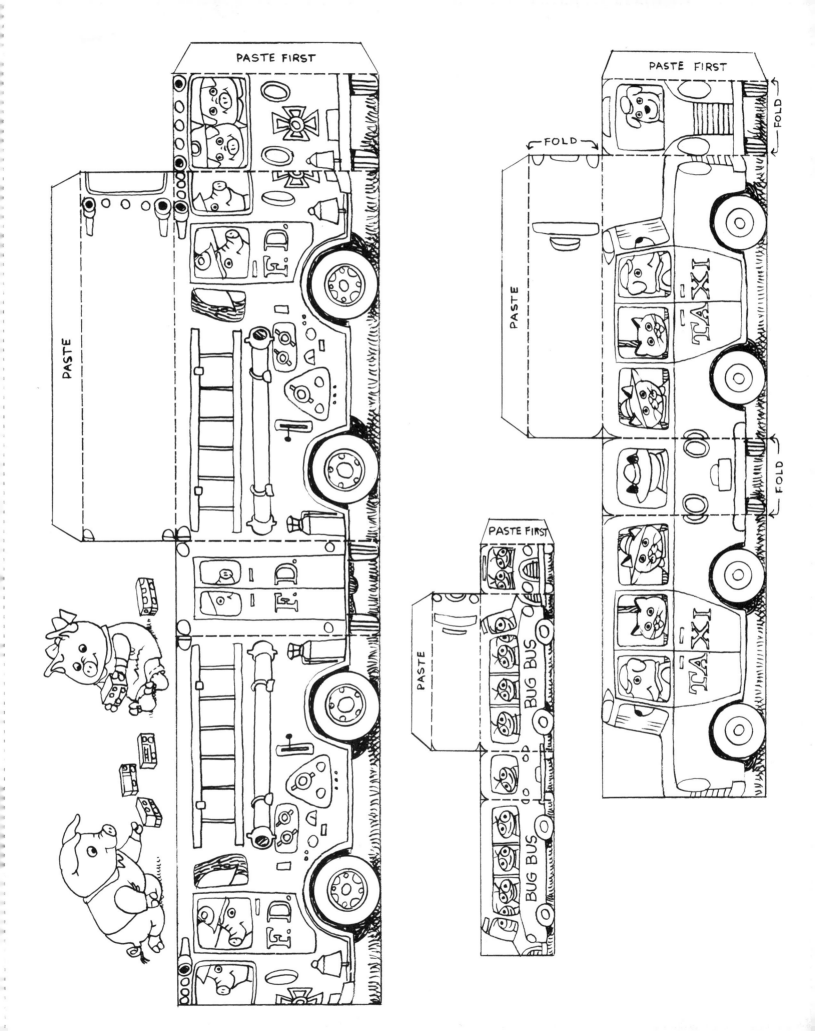

Remember—do your cutting on the other side of the page.

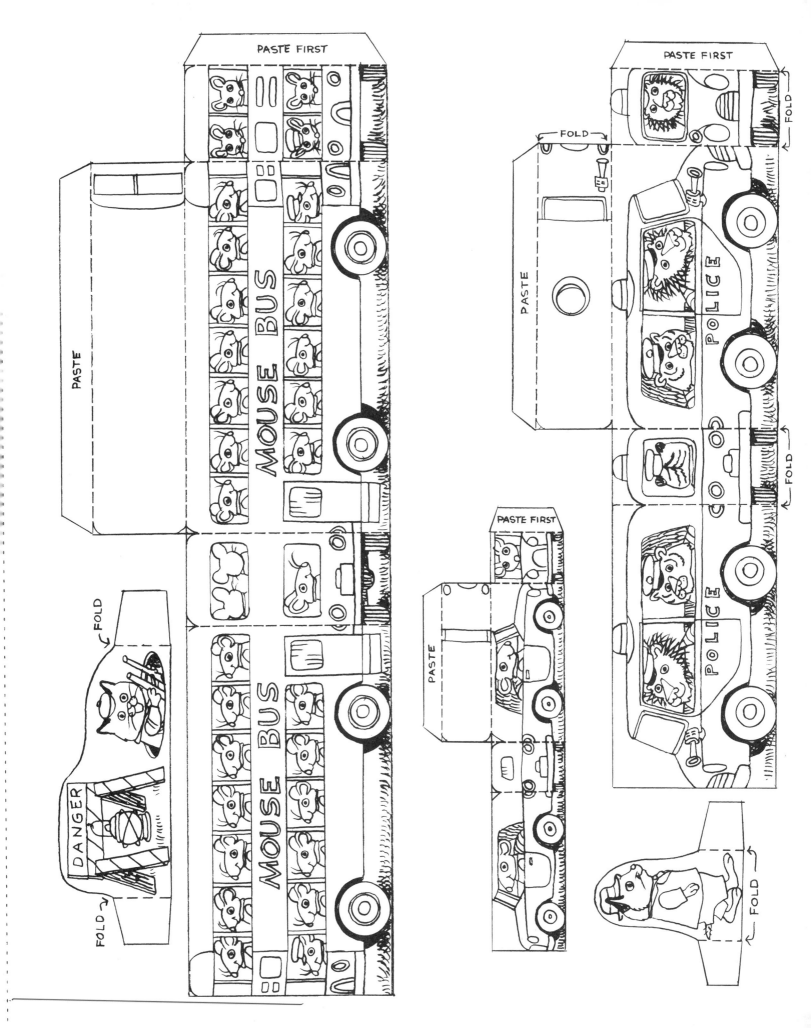

Remember—do your cutting on the other side of the page.

cargo boom

cargo winch

IRISH PENNANT

the ship's painter

KEEP OFF

dock

NUTS

WATER

FUEL OIL

EGGS

FRESH DAILY

APPLES

BREAD

CHEESE

MAIL

MAIL

The good ship IRISH PENNANT
is getting ready for a cruise.
Do you want to come along?

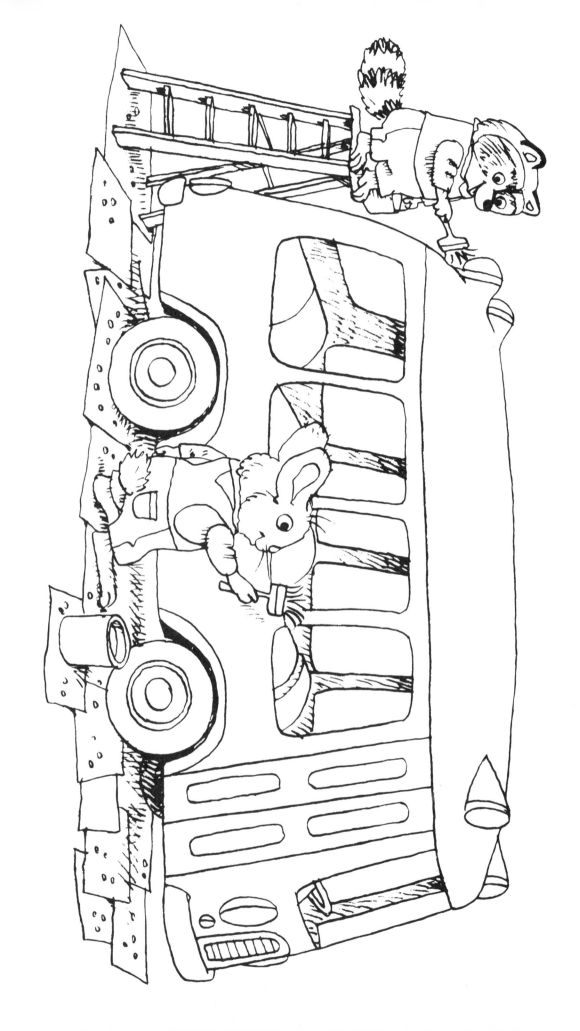

Help the animals paint the school bus.

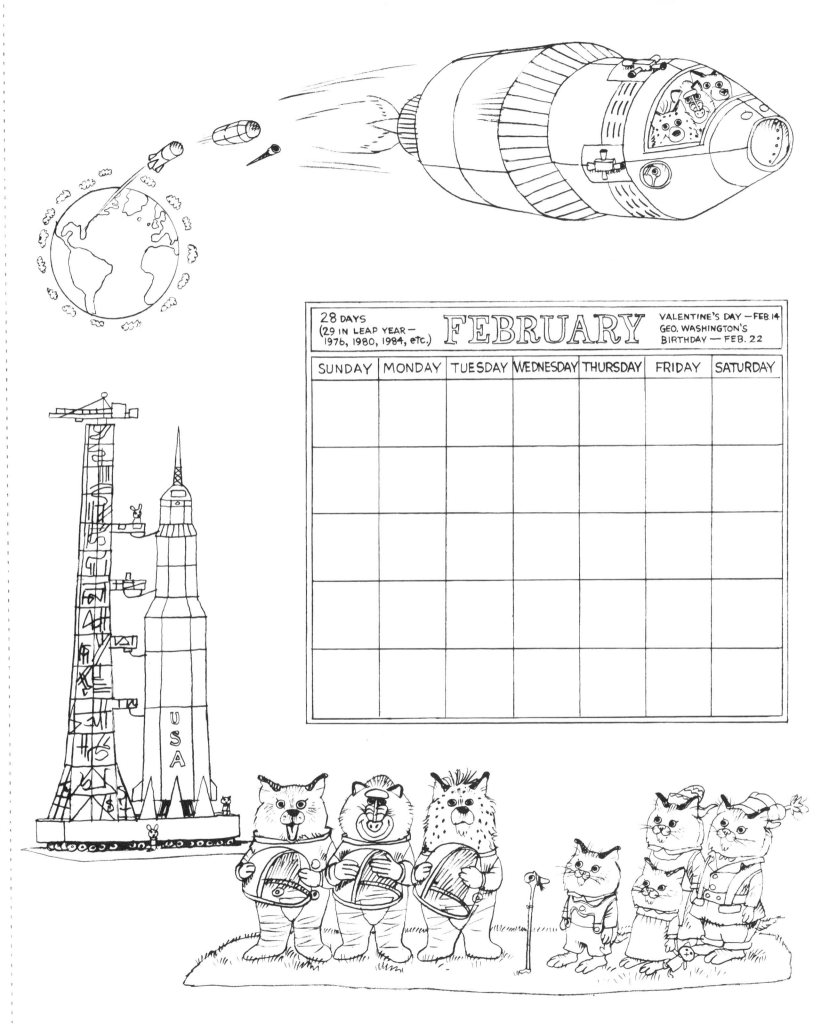

28 DAYS
(29 IN LEAP YEAR —
1976, 1980, 1984, etc.)

FEBRUARY

VALENTINE'S DAY — FEB.14
GEO. WASHINGTON'S
BIRTHDAY — FEB. 22

SUNDAY	MONDAY	TUESDAY	WEDNESDAY	THURSDAY	FRIDAY	SATURDAY

What are Huckle, Lowly, and Rudolf sitting in?
Connect the dots and find out.

VALENTINES

Harry Bear wants to say "I like you" to a friend on Valentine's Day, so he is making a valentine. You can make one, too.

Color the heart, front and back. Be sure to use some red. Go over the dotted lines of writing with a color. Fill in "To" and "From" on the back.

Cut out the heart, following the outline on this side of the page.

Oh, thank you!

Give your valentine on February 14.

Be My Valentine

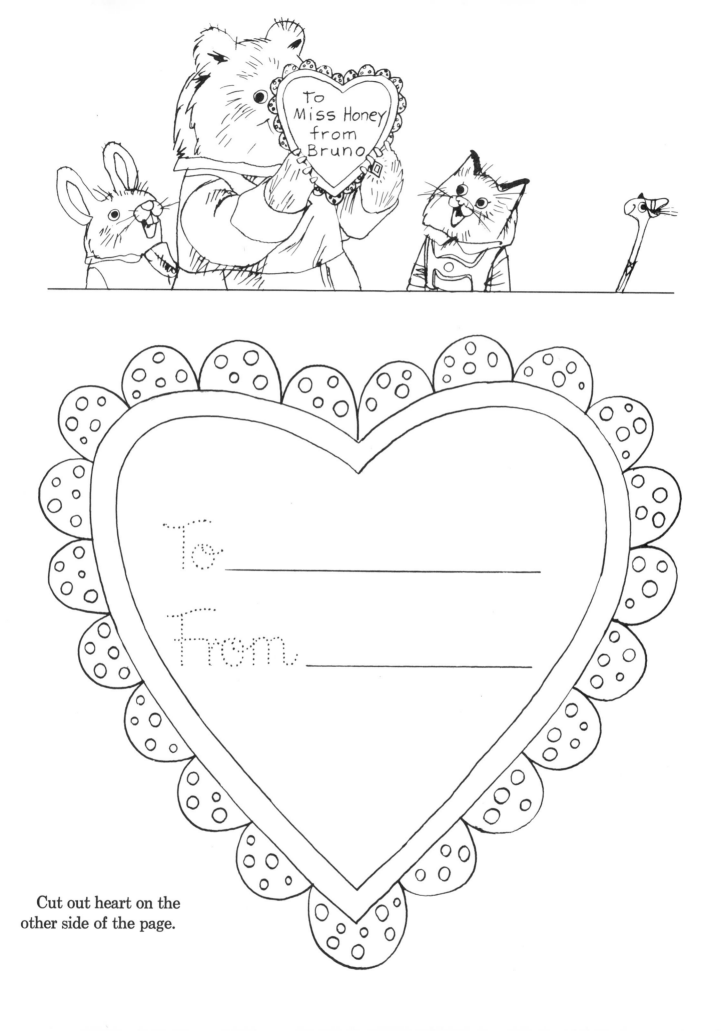

To Miss Honey from Bruno

To _____

From _____

Cut out heart on the other side of the page.

MORE VALENTINES

Color the cards, front and back.
Fill in "To" and "From" on the back.
Cut out the cards, following the
outline on this side of the page.

Here are some extra
hearts to color red.

Cut out your valentines on the other side of the page.

To _____

Roses are red, violets are blue
Sugar is sweet, and so are you!

FROM _____

To _____

FROM _____

Won't you be my valentine?

BE MY VALENTINE

To _____

FROM _____

Let's take a walk!

Help! Help!
Save Mother Cat!
Huckle, come down
from the attic
at once!

LADDER TRUCK

31 DAYS	MARCH				ST. PATRICK'S DAY — MAR. 17	
SUNDAY	MONDAY	TUESDAY	WEDNESDAY	THURSDAY	FRIDAY	SATURDAY

What a big
birthday cake!

BIRTHDAY CARDS

Are you going to a birthday party? You can make your own card to go with your present.

Color the card, front and back.

Sign your name on the back.

Cut out the card, following the outline on this side of the page.

Slip your card under the ribbon on the birthday present.

Have a good time at the party!

Happy Birthday

Happy Birthday

FROM _____

HAPPY BIRTHDAY

FROM _____

FROM _____

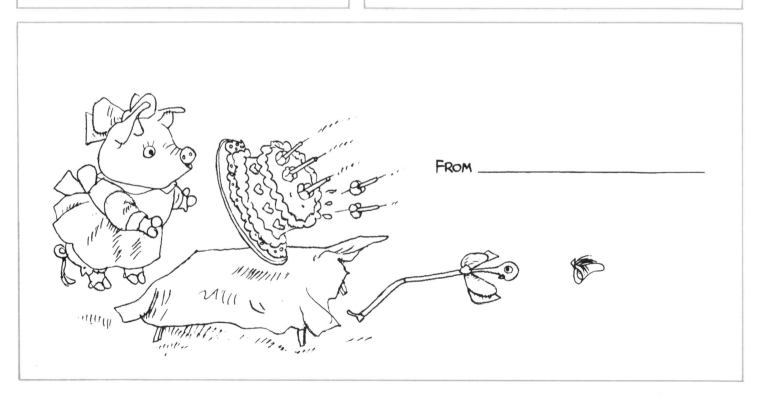

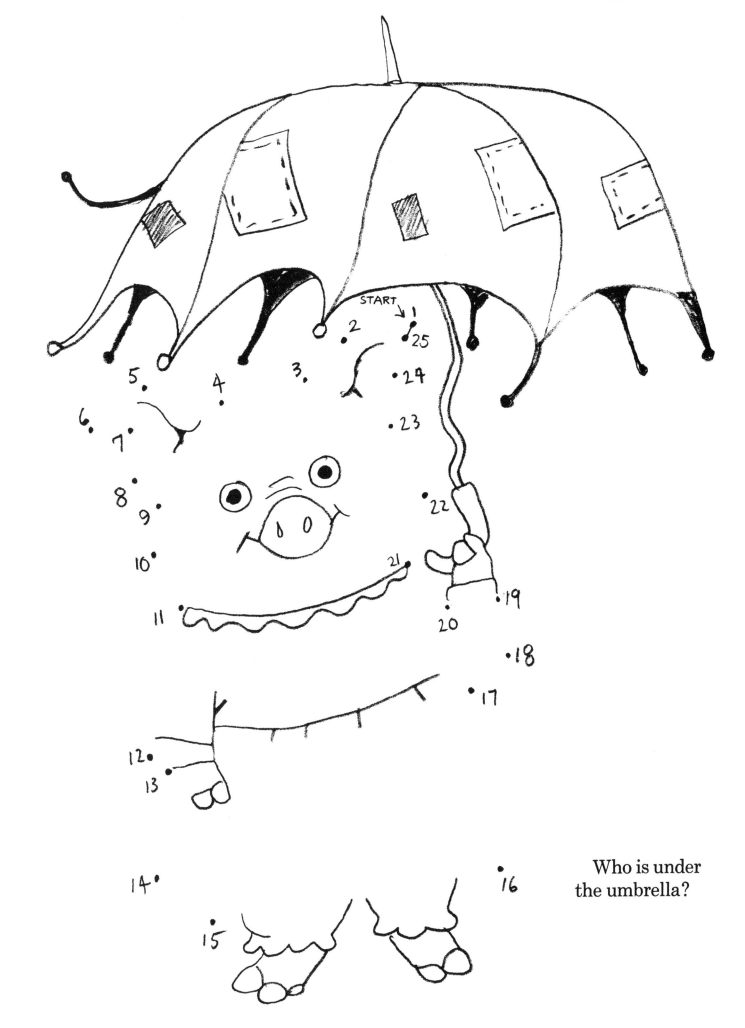

START

Who is under the umbrella?

Do you know how to play
Pin the Tail on the Donkey?

A PARTY GAME

Color the tails on the next page. Color the donkey on the page after next.

Cut out the tails along the black lines. Stick pins or thumbtacks through the "X" on the tails.

Tear out the whole donkey page. Tape or paste it on heavy paper or cardboard. Hang it on the wall.

Each player takes a tail. Each one is blind-folded in turn and tries to pin the tail on the correct place on the donkey. Whoever comes closest to the "X" is the winner.

You can make the game even harder if you like. Have the blindfolded player stand 6 or 8 feet from the donkey. Turn the player around 3 times, then point him in the direction of the donkey. He will be lucky to hit the donkey at all!

PARTY PLACE CARDS

Place cards tell your party guests where to sit at the table.

Color the cards on the next page. Write the name of each of your guests on a card. (Write your own name on a card, too!)

Cut out the cards along the solid black lines. Fold back the tabs along the dotted lines.

Stand a card at each person's place at the table.

Doesn't the table look nice?

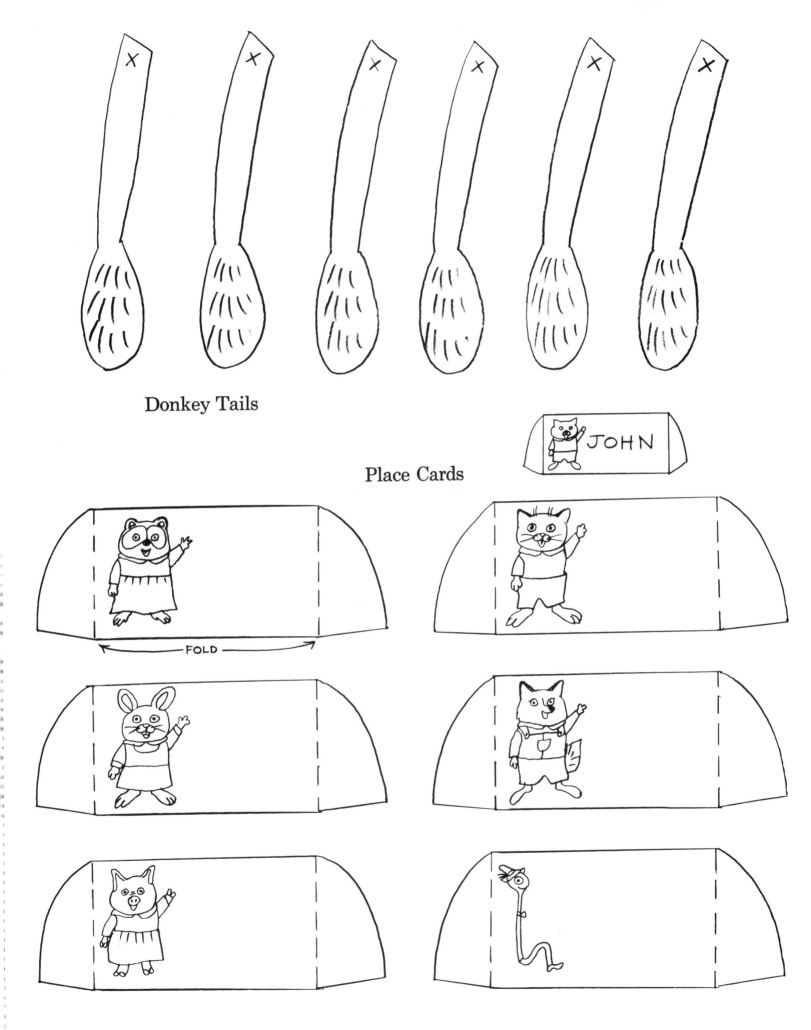

Donkey Tails

Place Cards

FOLD

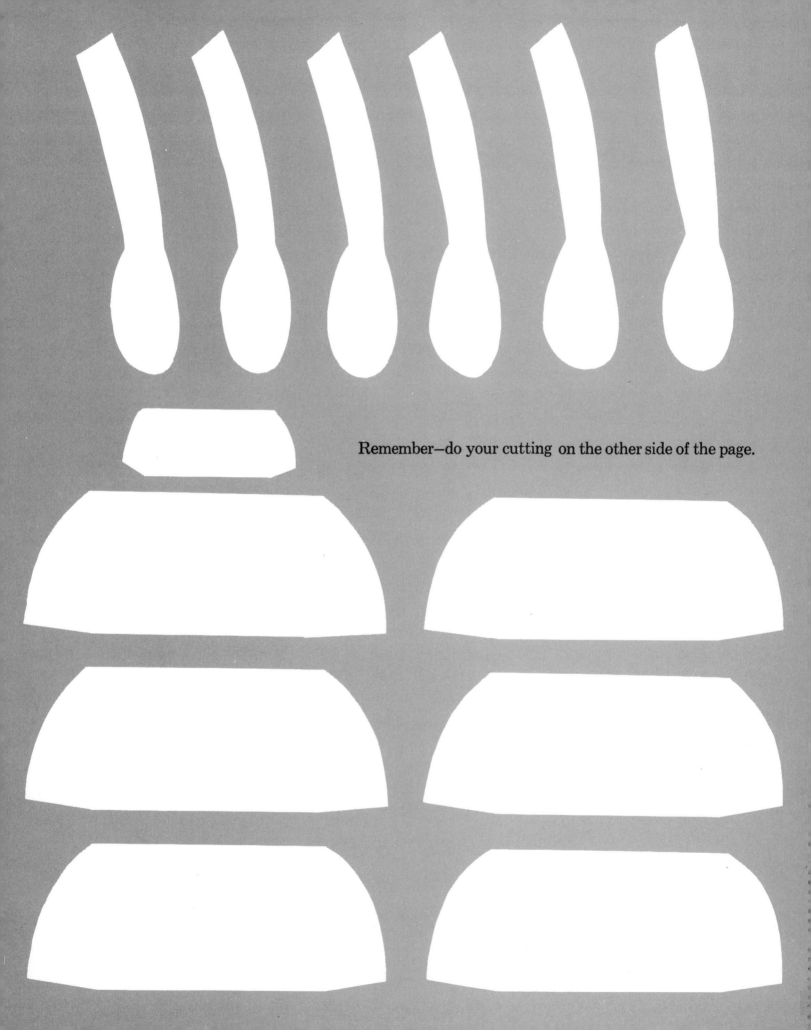

Remember—do your cutting on the other side of the page.

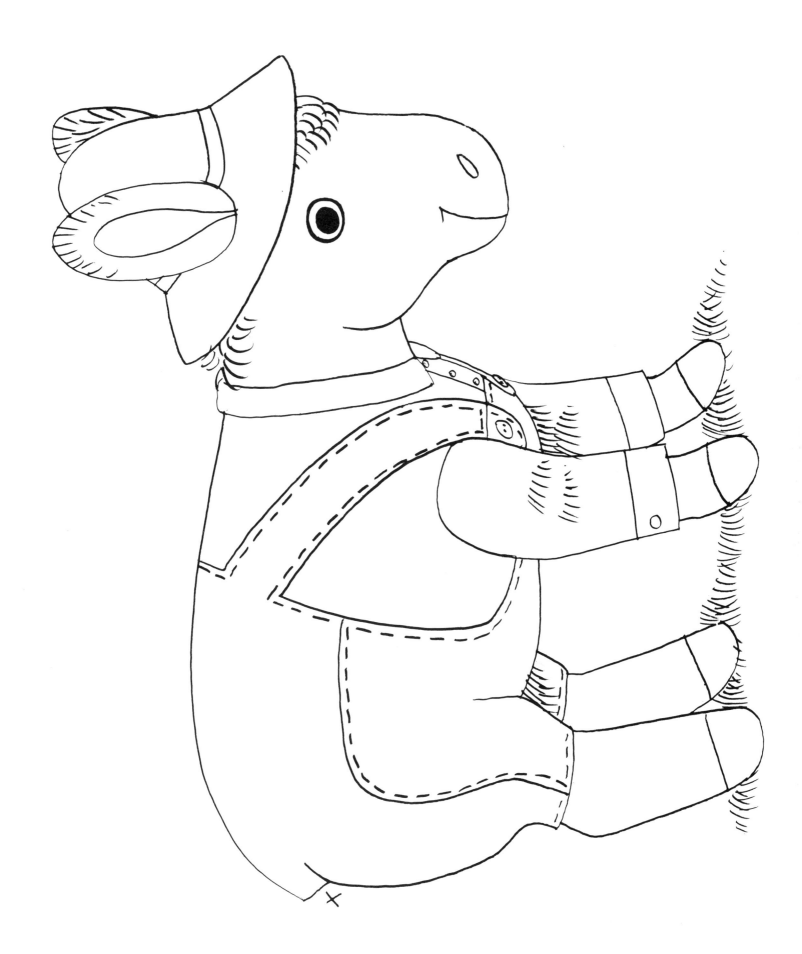

PASTE WHOLE PAGE

a Jet pilot

a poet
writing poems

an artist painting a picture   a story writer

a pretty model   a businessman   a violinist

a photographer   a secretary   an operator

CAFÉ

THE NEWS

THE REMARKABLE BOOK SHOP
E. KRAMER, PROP.

a book printer · a newspaper editor   a saleslady

a newspaper reporter   a janitor

Busy people in Busy Town

MAKING A PAPER AIRPLANE

Color the airplane on both sides of the next page.
Tear the whole page out. Fold along the dotted lines as shown below.

Now you are ready to fly!

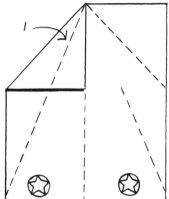

Fold down one top corner.

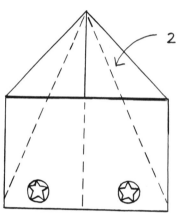

Fold down the other top corner.

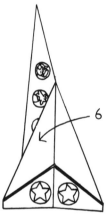

Fold again along the left diagonal dotted line.

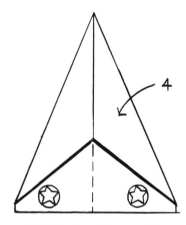

Fold along the right diagonal dotted line.

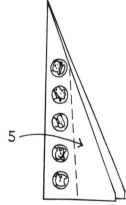

Fold along the center line.

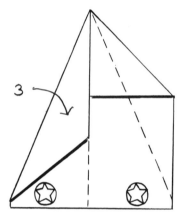

Fold back one wing.

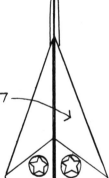

Fold down the other wing.

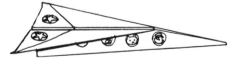

Here is the finished airplane. Hold the nose of the plane together and throw! Sometimes the plane flies best when you bend up the wing tips.

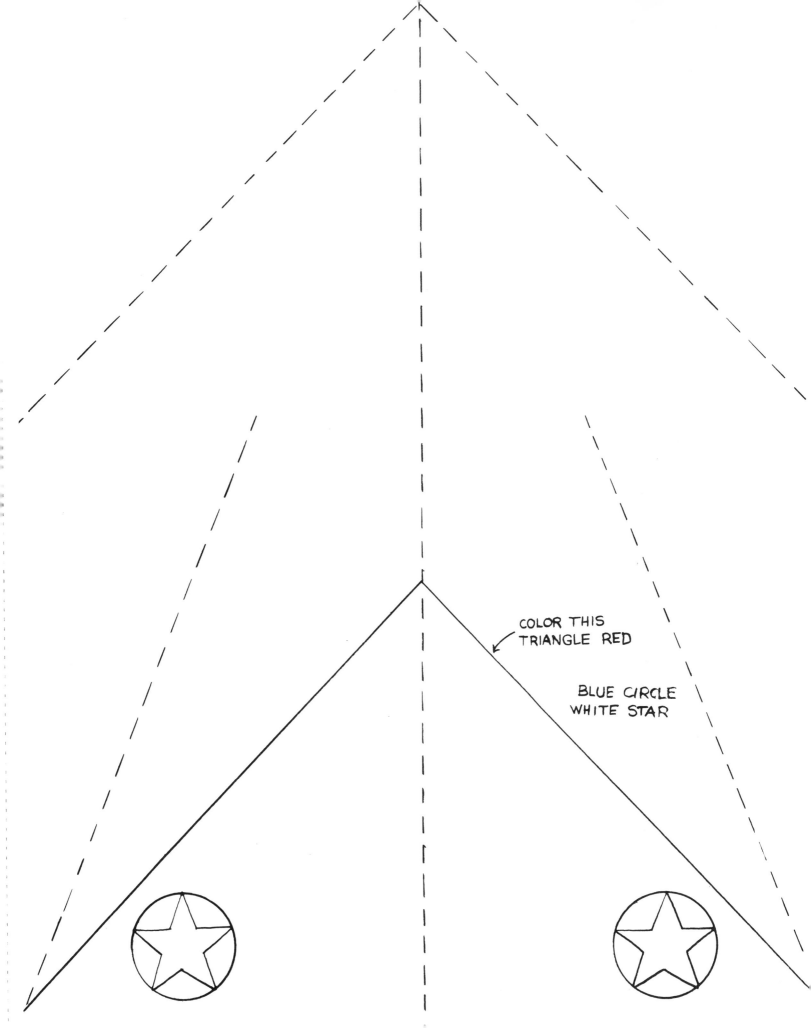

COLOR THIS
TRIANGLE RED

BLUE CIRCLE
WHITE STAR

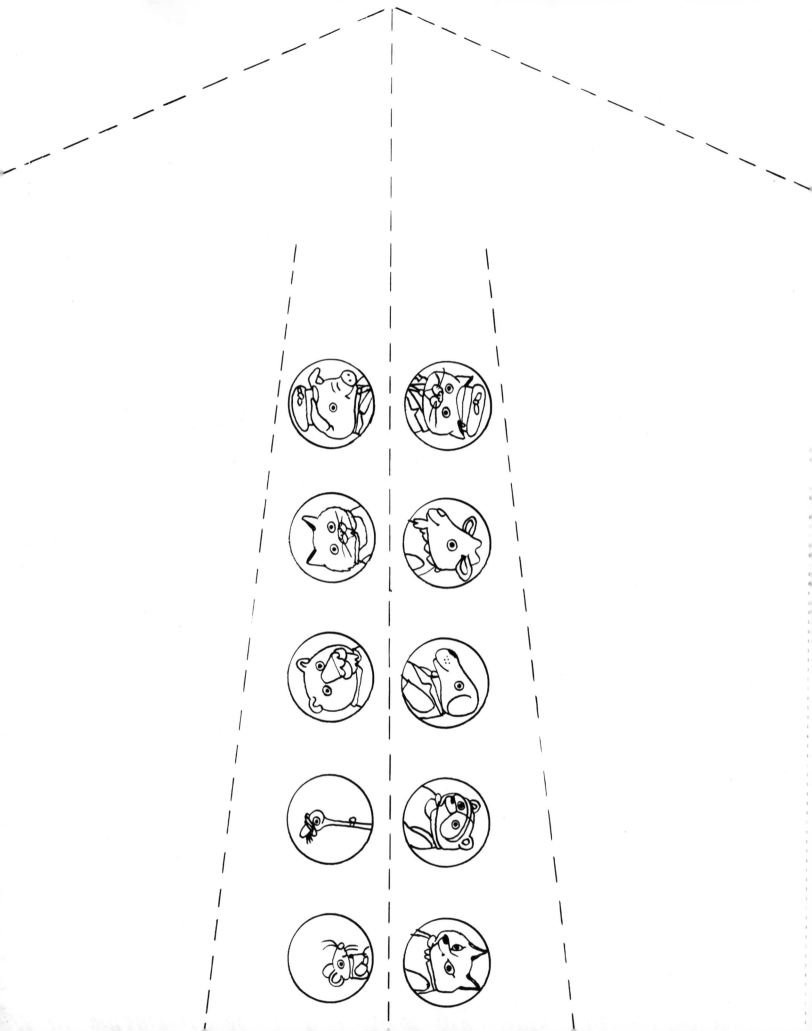

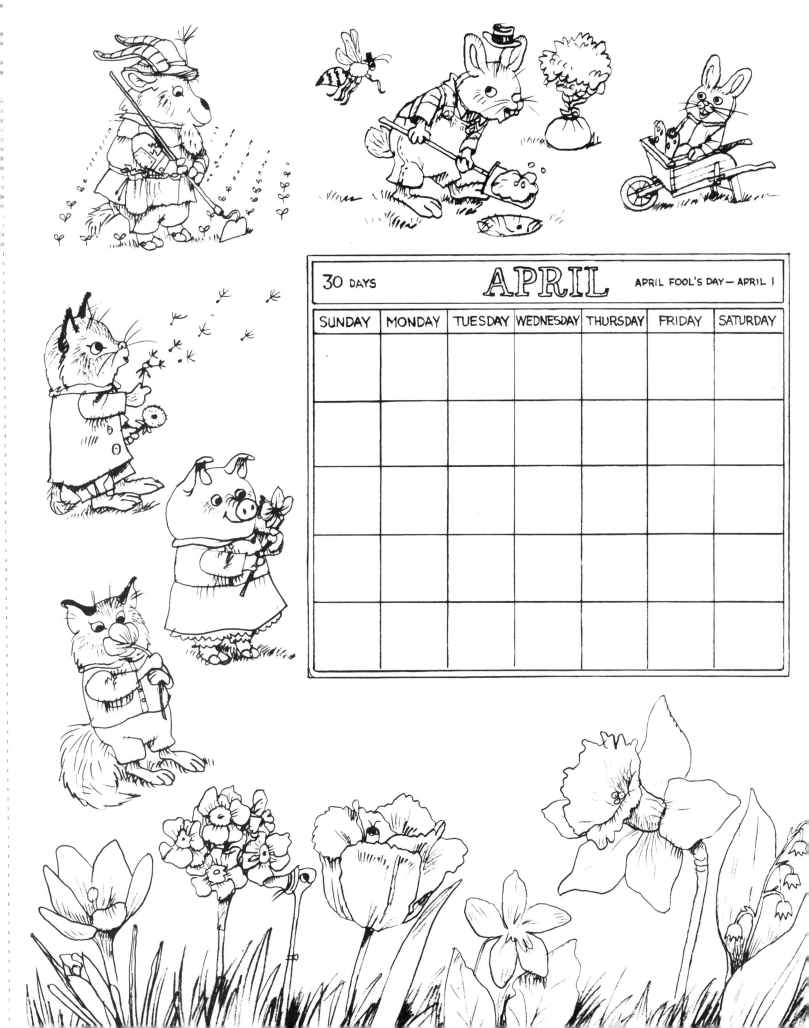

30 DAYS	APRIL				APRIL FOOL'S DAY — APRIL 1	
SUNDAY	MONDAY	TUESDAY	WEDNESDAY	THURSDAY	FRIDAY	SATURDAY

START

What has Huckle just seen?
Connect the dots.

EASTER TABLE DECORATION

Easter comes in March or April. The date is different every year. Ask your mother or father to tell you when Easter is this year. Then you will know when to make this Easter decoration.

Color the Easter bunny. Cut him out along the solid black outline. Fold back the tabs along the dotted lines to make him stand up.

Color the chicks on the next page, cut them out, and fold their tabs. Stand them up with the bunny on the table.

You can also use the chicks to decorate Easter eggs. Tape the tabs to hard-boiled eggs.

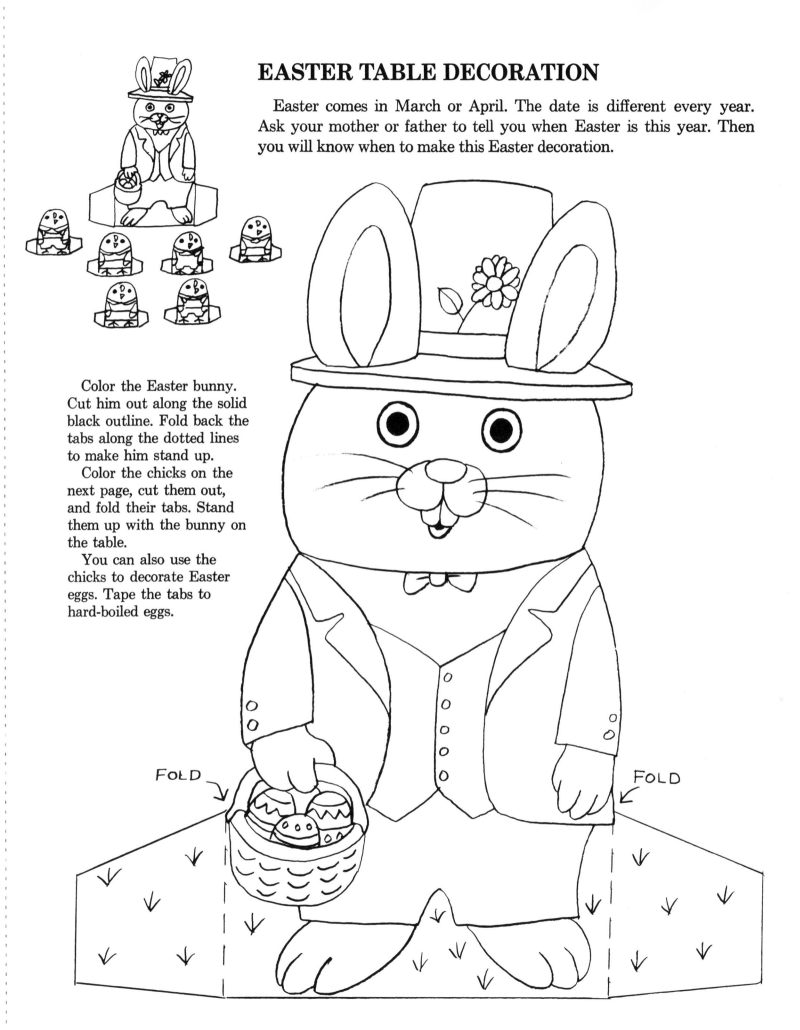

FOLD

FOLD

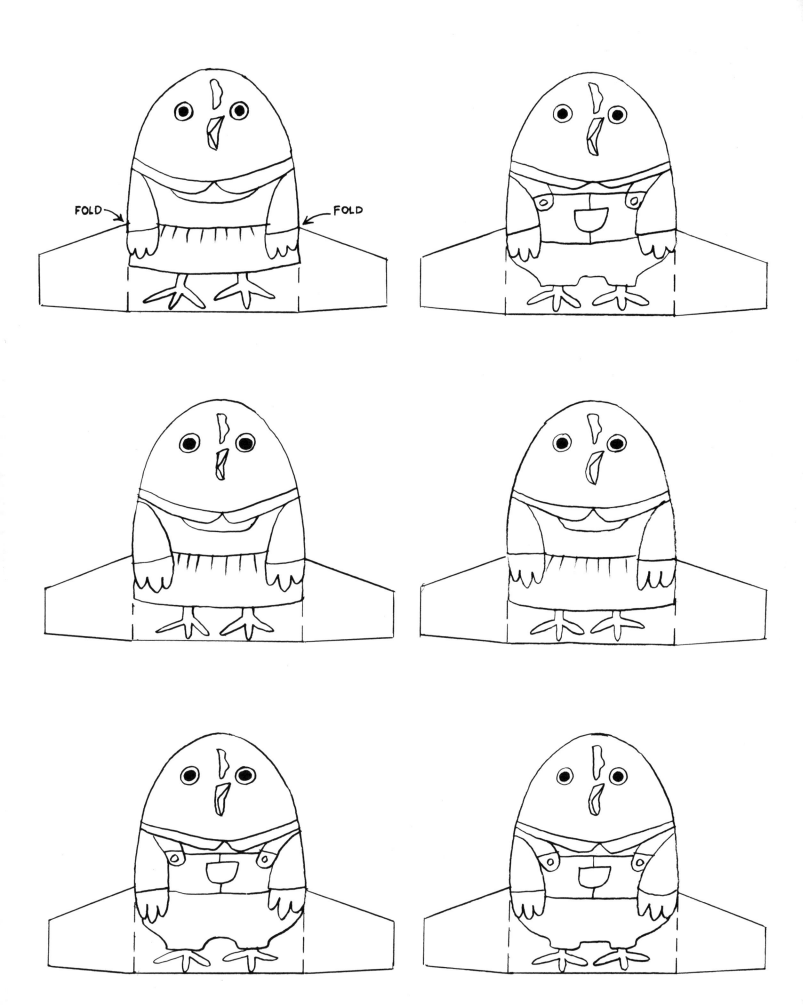

FOLD

FOLD

Remember—do your cutting on the other side of the page.

DETECTIVES IN DISGUISE

Sam and Dudley are detectives. They often wear disguises when they are solving mysteries. Then no one knows who they really are!

Sometimes they disguise themselves as sailors. Sometimes they even dress up as ladies!

Color Sam and Dudley. Then cut them out along the black outlines. Fold back the tabs to make them stand up. If you want the dolls to be sturdier, paste them on heavy paper or light cardboard before cutting.

FOLD →

← FOLD →

← FOLD

SAM CAT

Costumes for Sam and Dudley are on the next 3 pages. Color them and cut them out. Then fold back the tabs and dress Sam and Dudley in their disguises.

DUDLEY PIG

Remember—do your cutting on the other side of the page.

SAM CAT

DUDLEY PIG

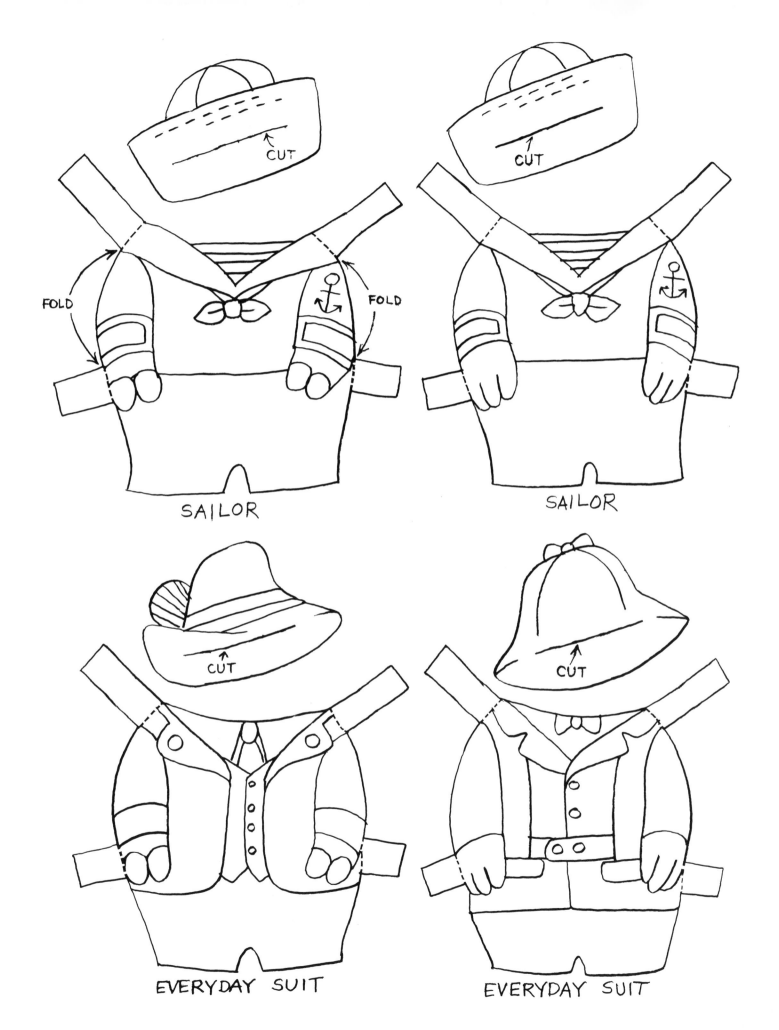

CUT

CUT

FOLD   FOLD

SAILOR

SAILOR

CUT

CUT

EVERYDAY SUIT

EVERYDAY SUIT

Do your cutting on
the other side of the page.

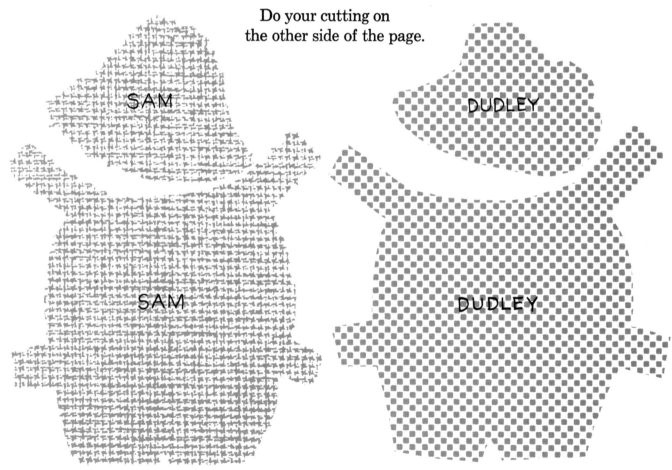

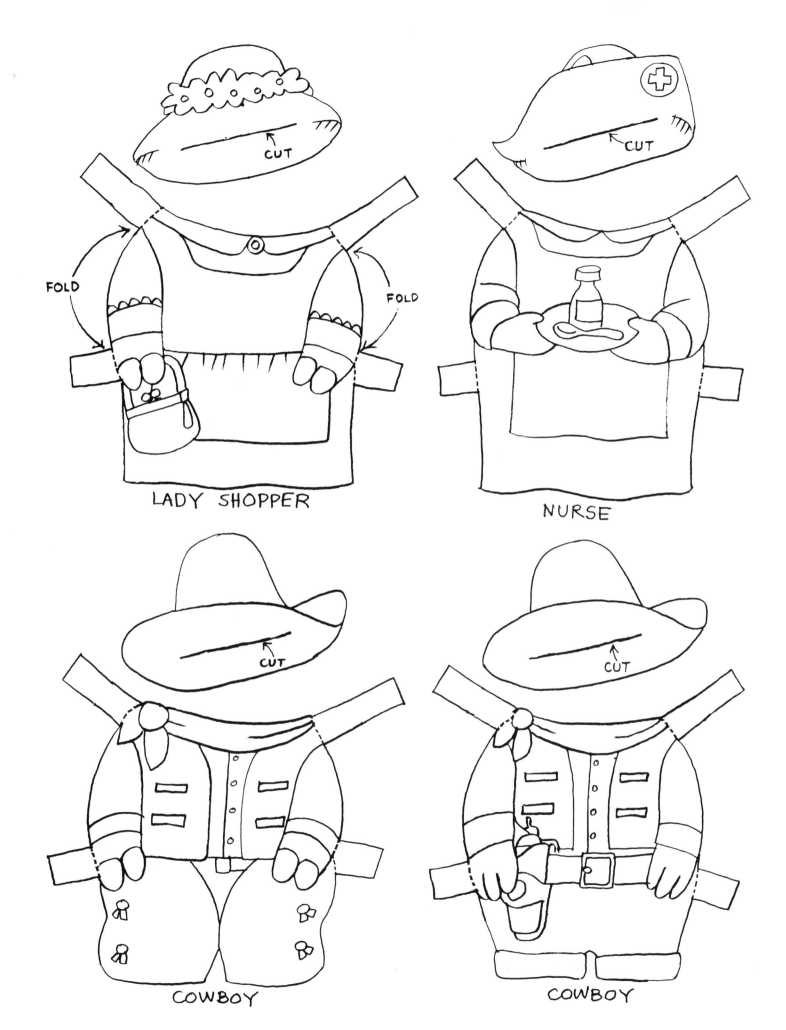

LADY SHOPPER

NURSE

COWBOY

COWBOY

Do your cutting on
the other side of the page.

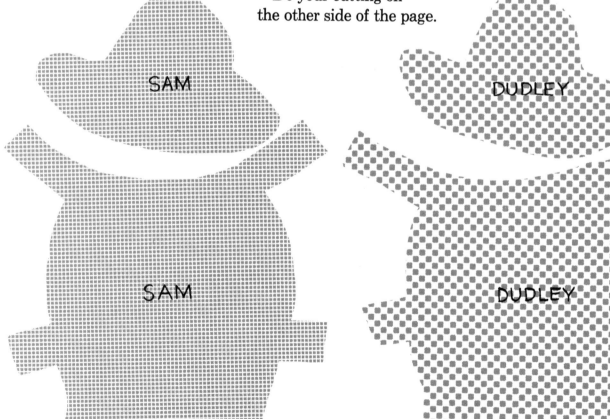

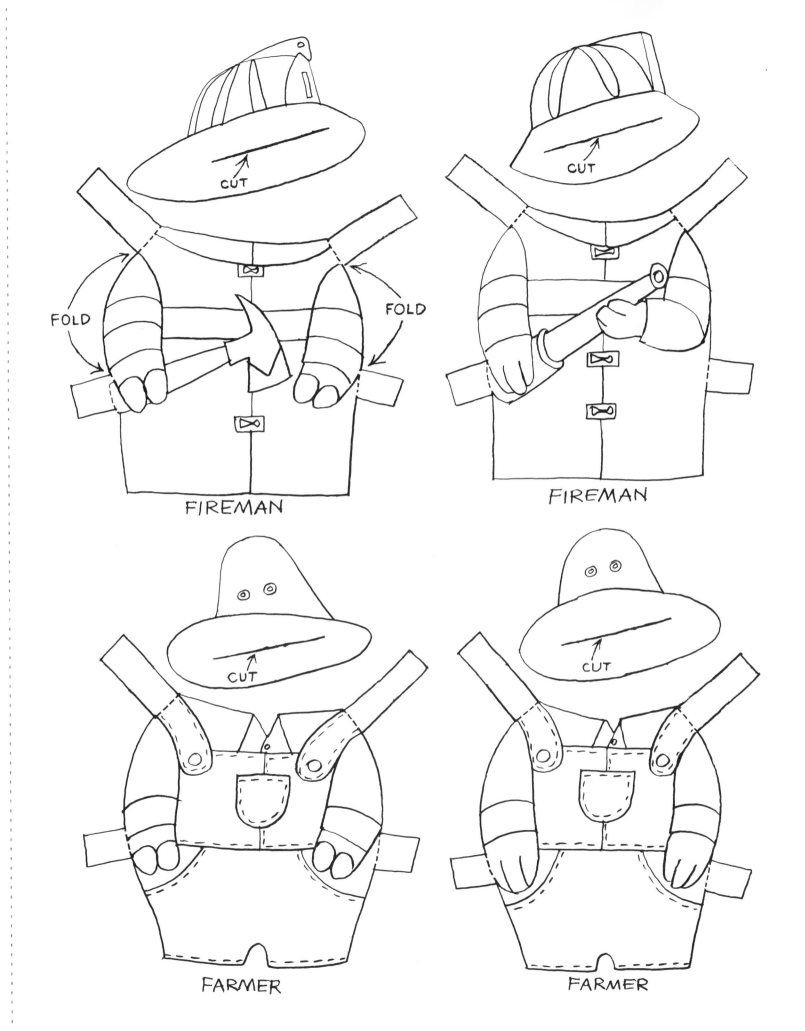

FIREMAN

FIREMAN

FARMER

FARMER

SAM

DUDLEY

SAM

DUDLEY

Do your cutting on
the other side of the page.

SAM

DUDLEY

SAM

DUDLEY

EASTER CARDS

Color the cards, front and back.
Fill in "To" and "From" on the back.
Cut the cards out, following the outlines on this side of the page.
Hand them out or mail them in envelopes.

Happy Easter

Happy Easter

HAPPY EASTER

Happy Easter!

Cut out Easter cards on the other side of the page.

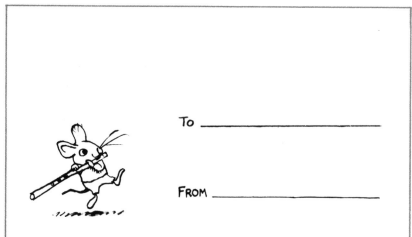

To _____

From _____

To _____

From _____

To _____

From _____

To _____

From _____

31 DAYS   MAY   MOTHER'S DAY — 2nd SUNDAY IN MAY
                  MEMORIAL DAY — LAST MONDAY IN MAY

SUNDAY	MONDAY	TUESDAY	WEDNESDAY	THURSDAY	FRIDAY	SATURDAY

7 8
6
4 5
3
2
1

What a tasty dinner!

FINGER PUPPETS

Color the finger puppets. Cut them out along the outlines.

Bend the tabs around two of your fingers and fasten them with sticky tape.

Wiggle your fingers to make the animals move their heads and talk to each other.

Remember—do your cutting on the other side of the page.

MOTHER'S DAY CARD

Mother's Day is the second Sunday in May. Here is a special card that you can make for your mother.

Color the pictures on the card, front and back. Then cut it out, following the outline on this side of the page. Fold along the dotted line.

Write your name for your mother (Mama, Mommy, etc.) on the front of the card. Sign your name inside.

← FOLD

Cut on the other side of the page.

Happy Mother's Day

FROM _____

Farmer Cat likes to drive his tractor.

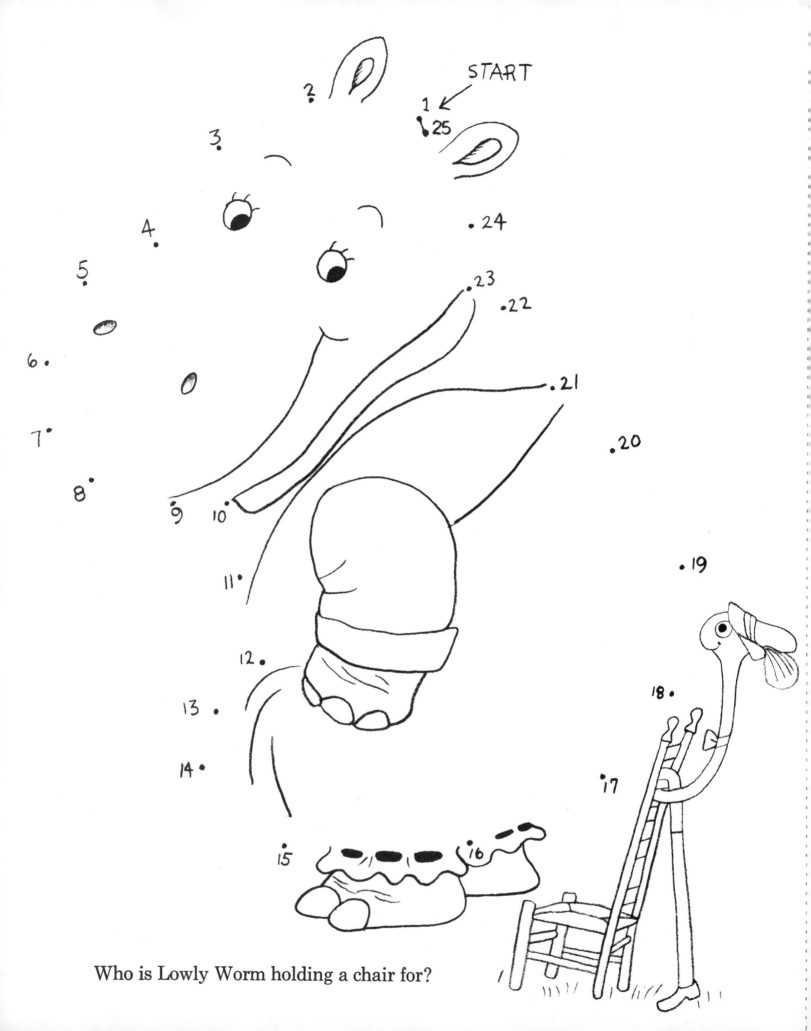

START

Who is Lowly Worm holding a chair for?

AIRPLANE MOBILE

Color the planes on this page and the next, on both sides.

Cut the planes out along the outlines.

Gently punch out holes with a pencil.

Tie the planes together with thread or string, just as the picture shows.

Hang them from a stick or wire coat hanger and watch them move in the breeze.

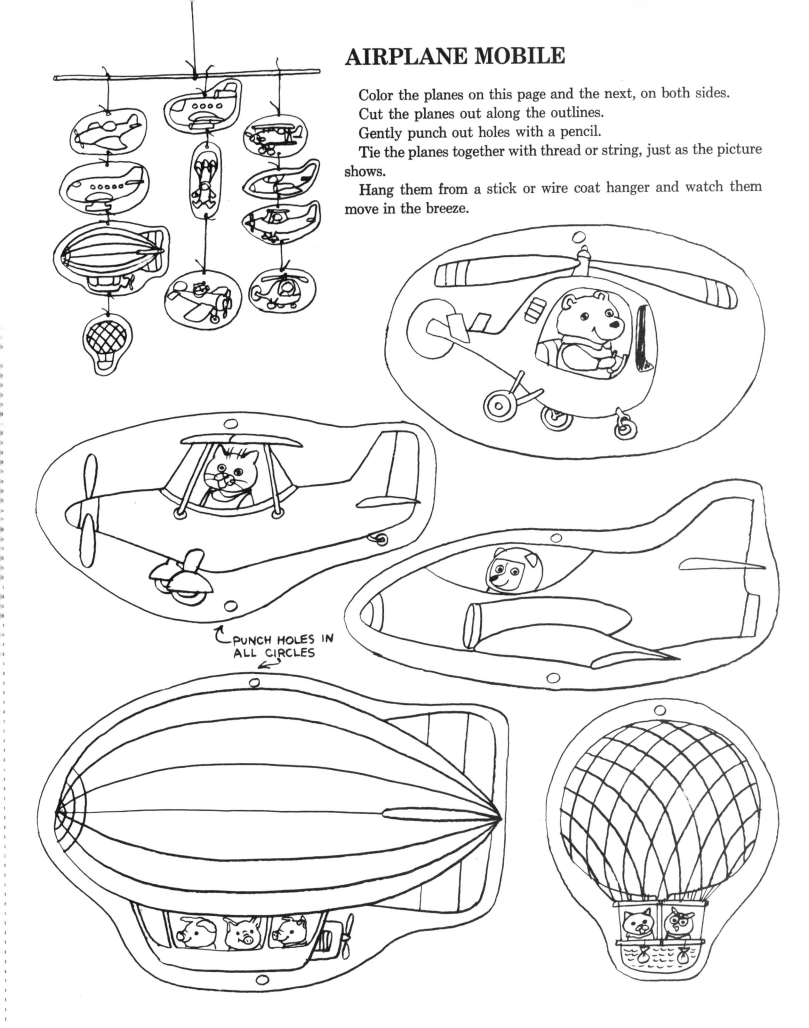

PUNCH HOLES IN
ALL CIRCLES

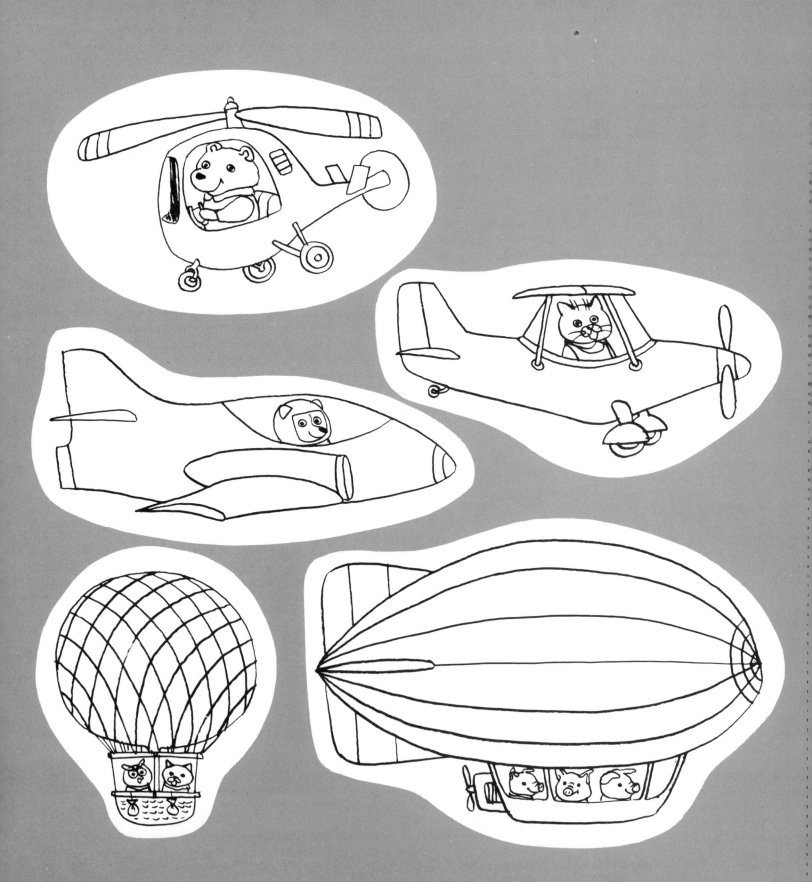

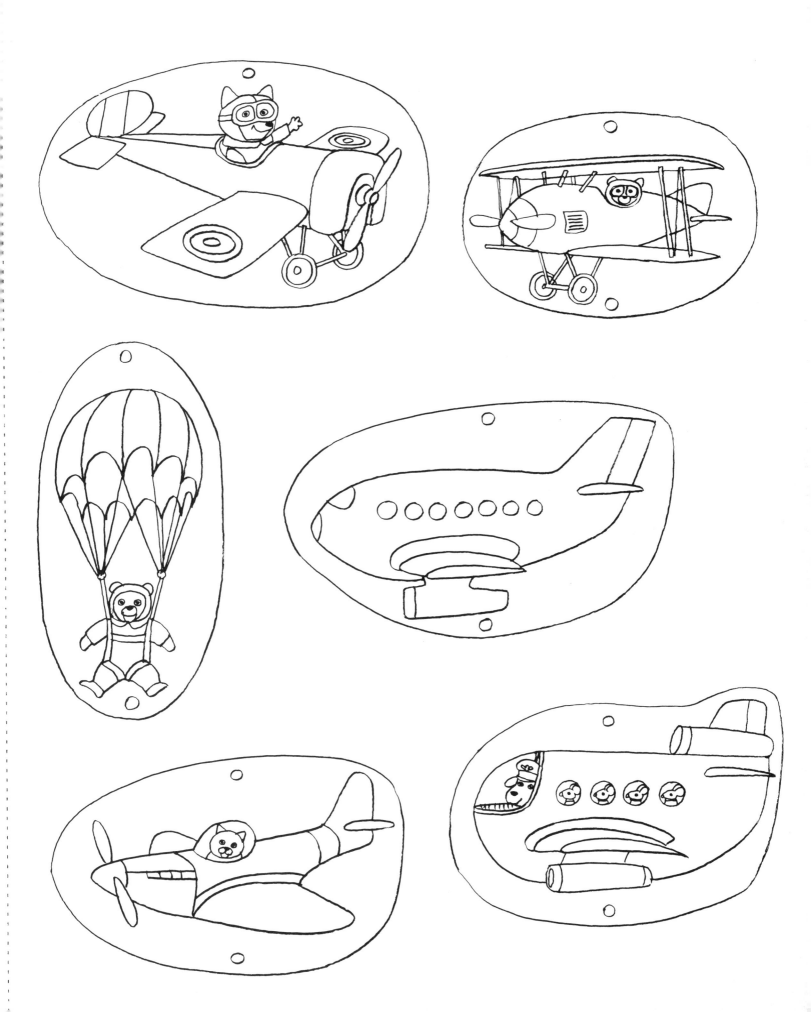

Do your cutting on the other side of the page.

A nice sunny day at the beach

bath house

1 2 3

beach umbrella

tent

doll

shovel

pail

sand castle

starfish

The Early Bird meets Bunny Rabbit.

runway

control tower

weather bureau

waiting room

observation deck

30 DAYS	JUNE			FATHER'S DAY — 3rd SUN. IN JUNE		
SUNDAY	MONDAY	TUESDAY	WEDNESDAY	THURSDAY	FRIDAY	SATURDAY
	moving Day					

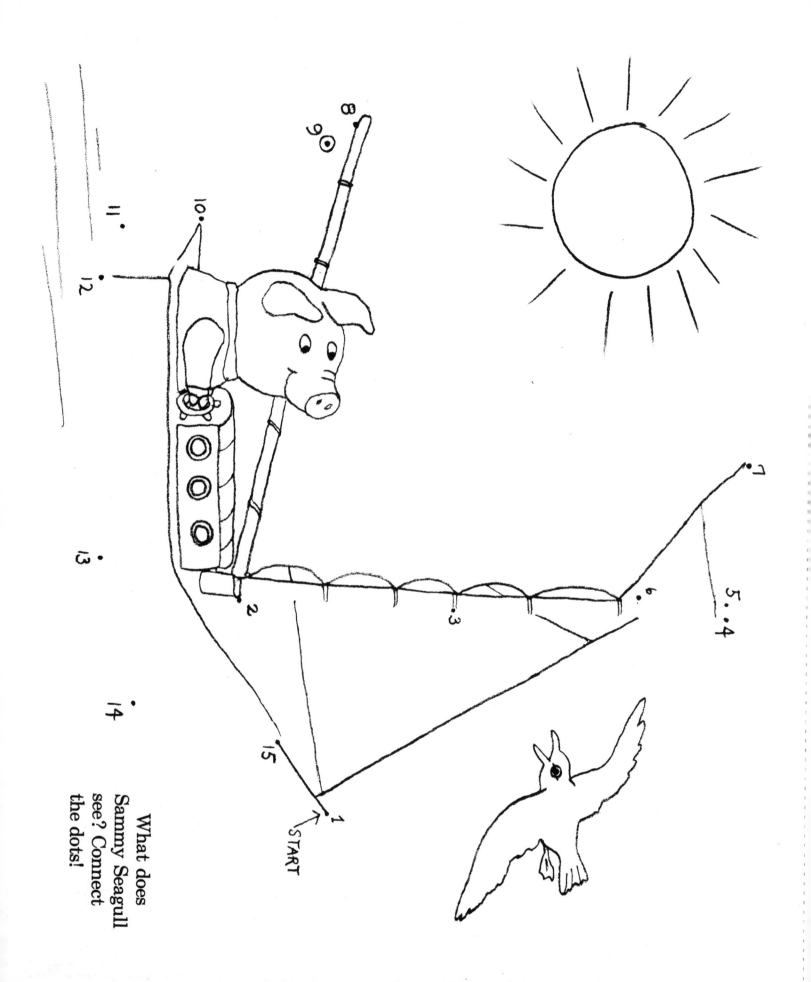

What does
Sammy Seagull
see? Connect
the dots!

START

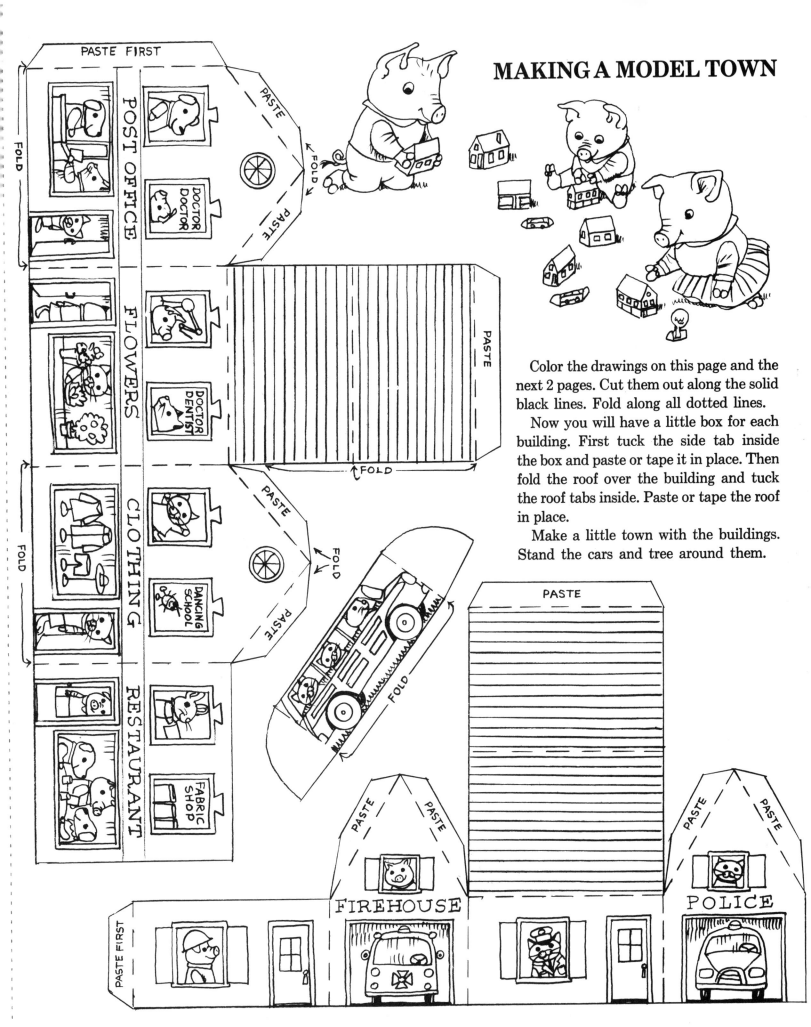

MAKING A MODEL TOWN

PASTE FIRST

FOLD

POST OFFICE

DOCTOR DOCTOR

PASTE

FOLD

PASTE

FLOWERS

DOCTOR DENTIST

PASTE

FOLD

CLOTHING

DANCING SCHOOL

FOLD

PASTE

FOLD

PASTE

RESTAURANT

FABRIC SHOP

FOLD

PASTE

Color the drawings on this page and the next 2 pages. Cut them out along the solid black lines. Fold along all dotted lines.

Now you will have a little box for each building. First tuck the side tab inside the box and paste or tape it in place. Then fold the roof over the building and tuck the roof tabs inside. Paste or tape the roof in place.

Make a little town with the buildings. Stand the cars and tree around them.

PASTE

PASTE

PASTE

PASTE

PASTE

PASTE FIRST

FIREHOUSE

POLICE

Remember—do your cutting on the other side of the page.

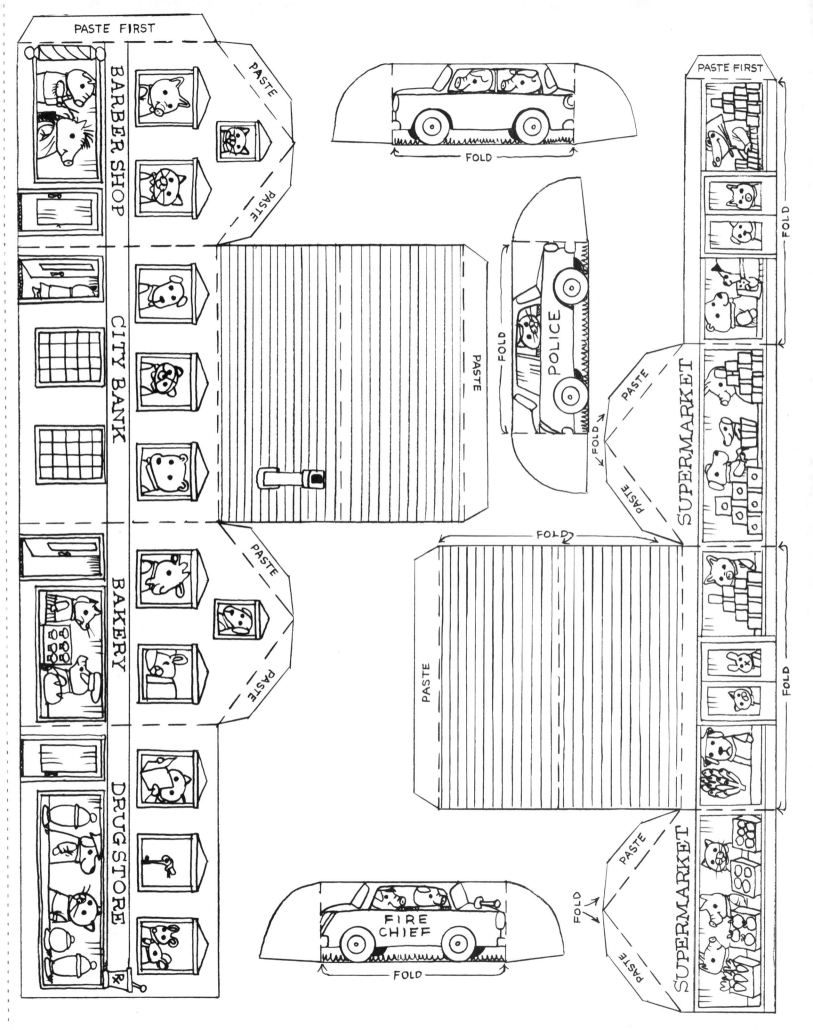

Remember—do your cutting on the other side of the page.

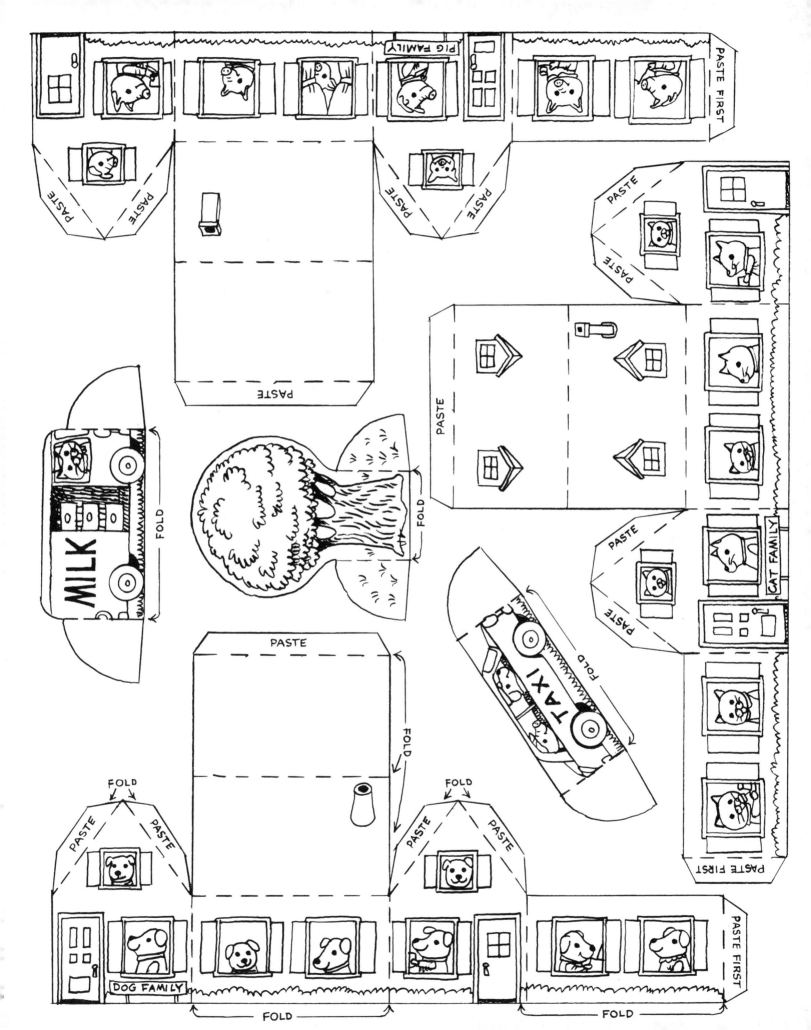

Remember—do your cutting
on the other side of the page.

FATHER'S DAY CARD

Father's Day is the third Sunday in June. Surprise your father with this funny card.

Color the pictures on the card, front and back.

Then cut it out, following the outline on this side of the page. Fold along the dotted line.

Write your name for your father (Papa, Daddy, etc.) on the front of the card. Sign your name inside.

Cut out card on the other side of the page.

Happy Father's Day

FROM _____

31 DAYS	JULY			INDEPENDENCE DAY — JULY 4		
SUNDAY	MONDAY	TUESDAY	WEDNESDAY	THURSDAY	FRIDAY	SATURDAY

ICE CREAM

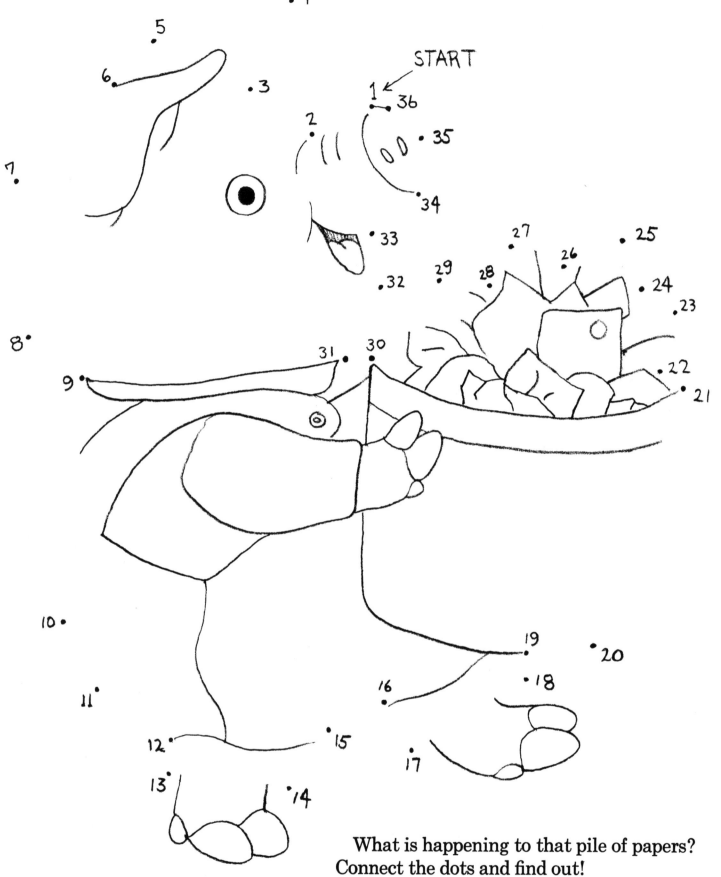

START

What is happening to that pile of papers?
Connect the dots and find out!

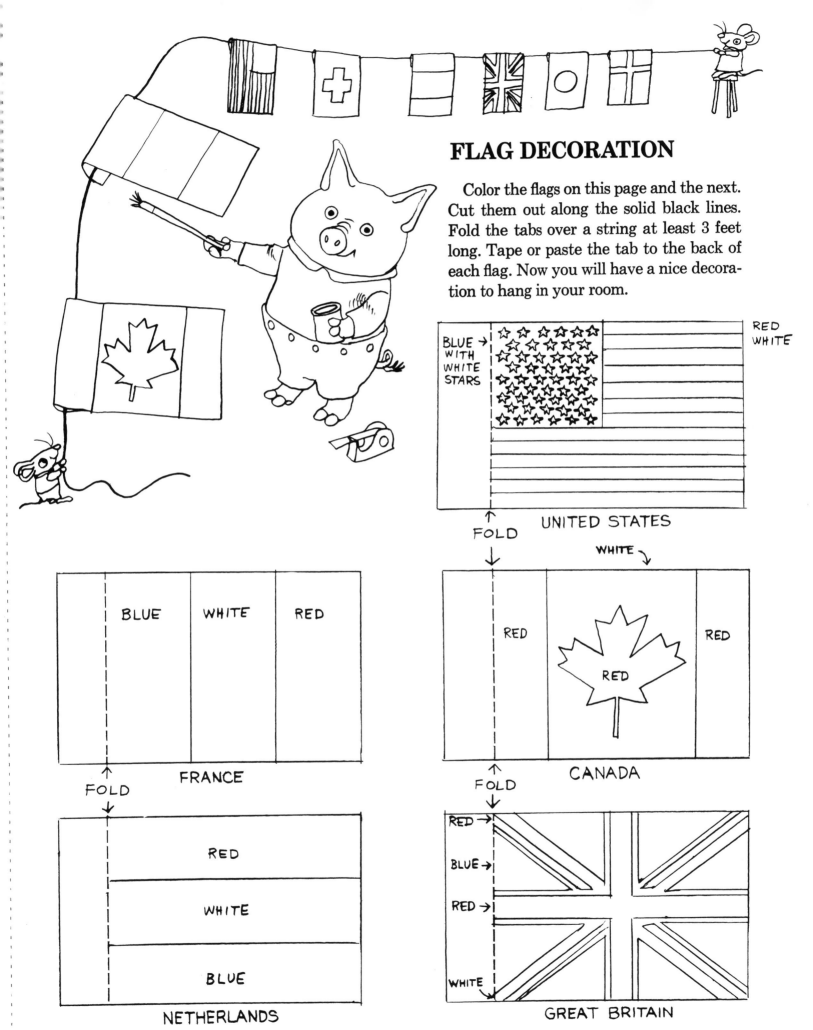

FLAG DECORATION

Color the flags on this page and the next. Cut them out along the solid black lines. Fold the tabs over a string at least 3 feet long. Tape or paste the tab to the back of each flag. Now you will have a nice decoration to hang in your room.

RED
WHITE

BLUE →
WITH
WHITE
STARS

FOLD

UNITED STATES

BLUE   WHITE   RED

FOLD

FRANCE

WHITE ↘

RED

RED

RED

FOLD

CANADA

RED

WHITE

BLUE

NETHERLANDS

FOLD

RED →
BLUE →
RED →

WHITE

GREAT BRITAIN

Do your cutting on the other side of the page.

UNITED STATES

PASTE

CANADA

PASTE

FRANCE

PASTE

GREAT BRITAIN

PASTE

NETHERLANDS

PASTE

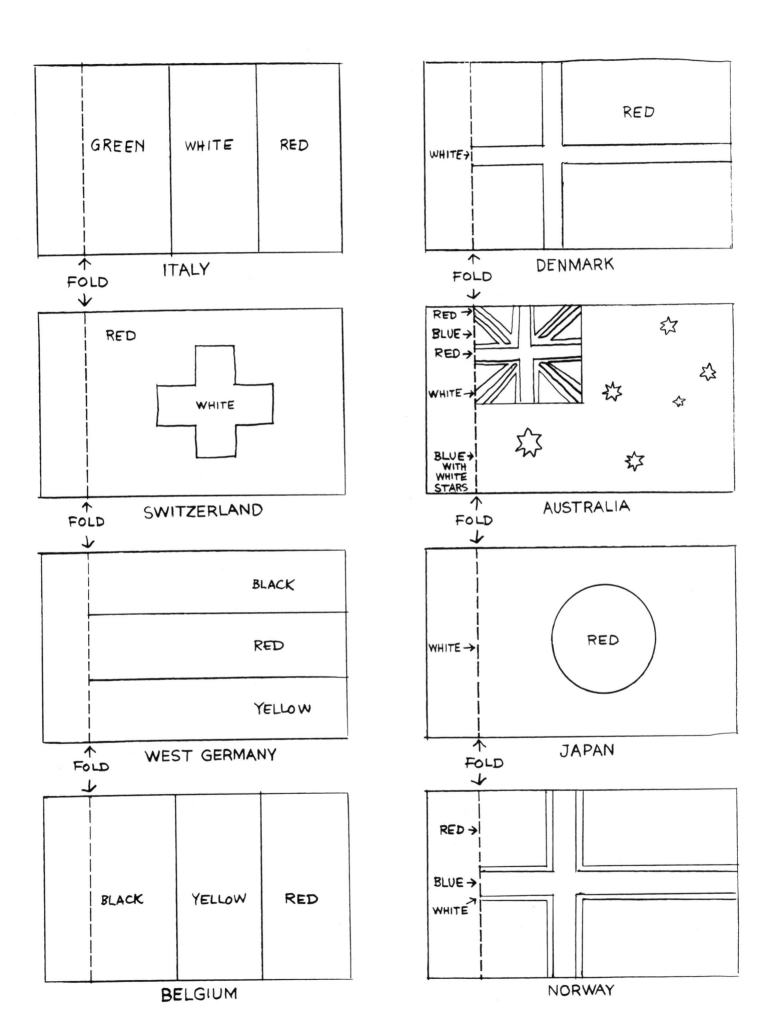

GREEN WHITE RED

ITALY

FOLD

RED

WHITE

SWITZERLAND

FOLD

BLACK

RED

YELLOW

WEST GERMANY

FOLD

BLACK YELLOW RED

BELGIUM

WHITE →

RED

DENMARK

FOLD

RED →
BLUE →
RED →

WHITE →

BLUE →
WITH
WHITE
STARS

AUSTRALIA

FOLD

WHITE →

RED

JAPAN

FOLD

RED →

BLUE →

WHITE →

NORWAY

Do your cutting on the other side of the page.

DENMARK

PASTE

ITALY

PASTE

AUSTRALIA

PASTE

SWITZERLAND

PASTE

JAPAN

PASTE

WEST GERMANY

PASTE

NORWAY

PASTE

BELGIUM

PASTE

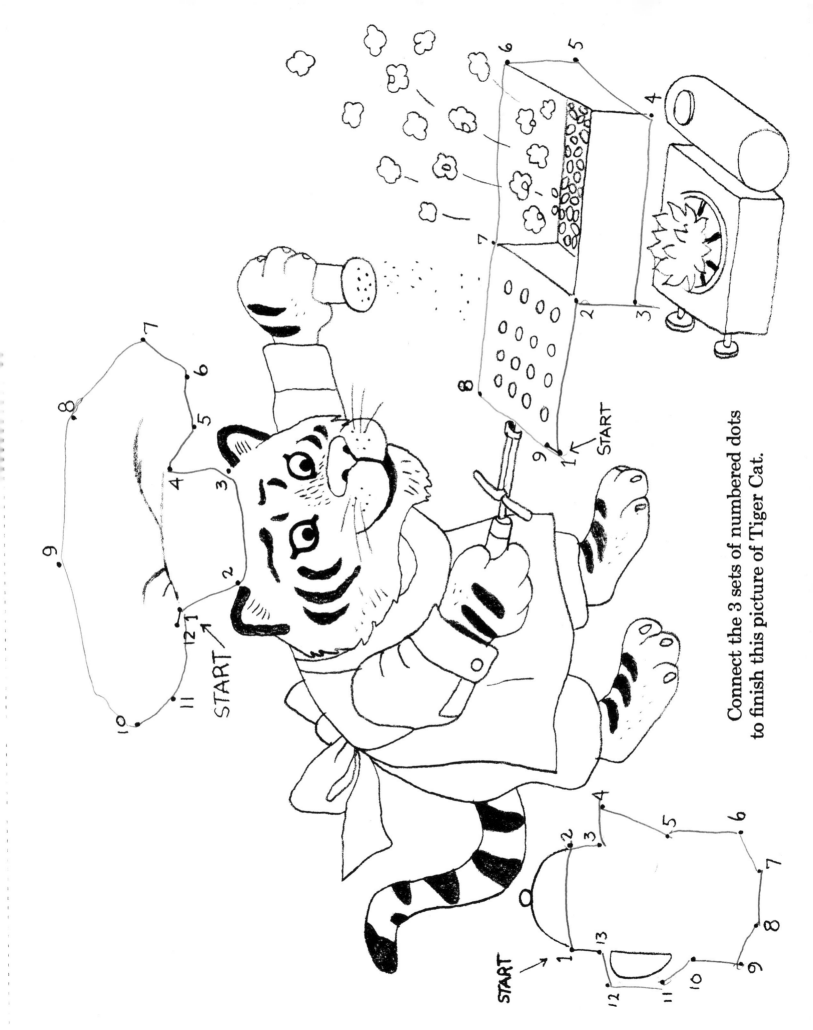

Connect the 3 sets of numbered dots to finish this picture of Tiger Cat.

HOW TO MAKE TWO FLYING CROWS

Color Ma and Pa Crow on the next two pages, on both sides of each page. Use lots of different colors.

Tear out both pages along the perforated lines.

Fold the crows along the dotted lines, as shown below.

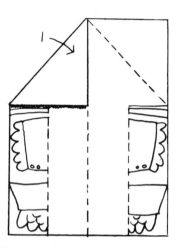

Start with the side of the paper that doesn't show the eyes. Fold down one top corner.

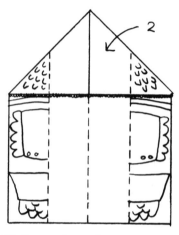

Fold down the other top corner.

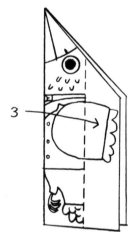

Fold along the center dotted line.

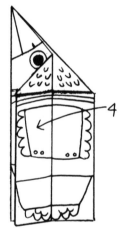

Fold over the top wing.

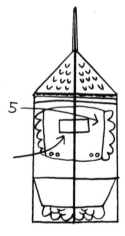

Fold the other wing. Fasten the two wings together with sticky tape.

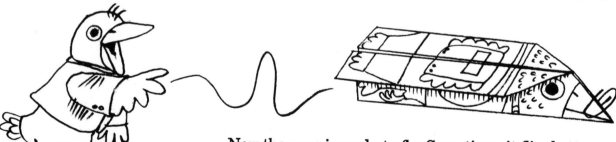

Now the crow is ready to fly. Sometimes it flies better if the beak is held together with a paper clip.

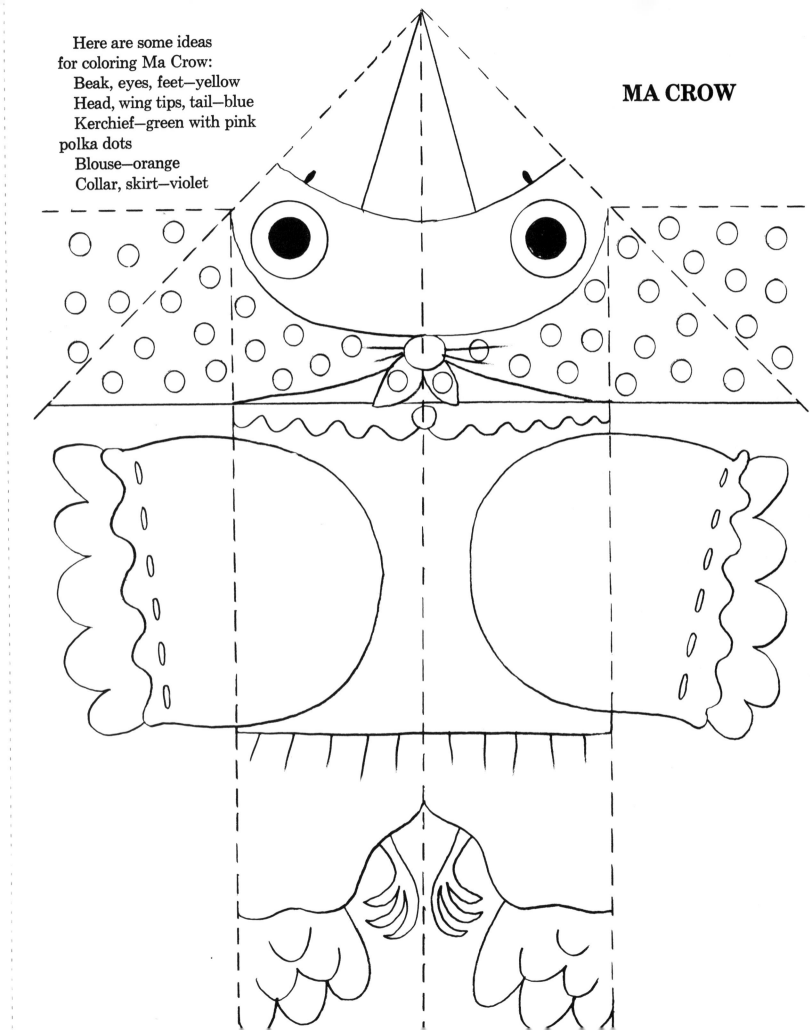

Here are some ideas
for coloring Ma Crow:
   Beak, eyes, feet—yellow
   Head, wing tips, tail—blue
   Kerchief—green with pink
polka dots
   Blouse—orange
   Collar, skirt—violet

MA CROW

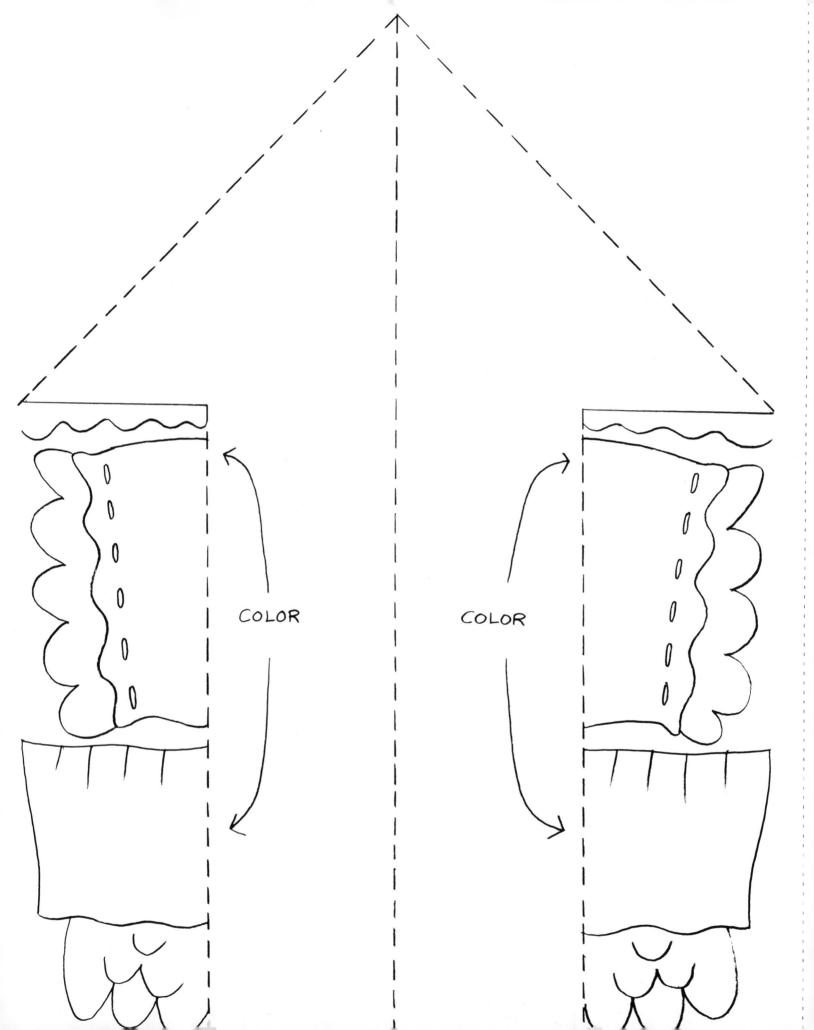

COLOR

COLOR

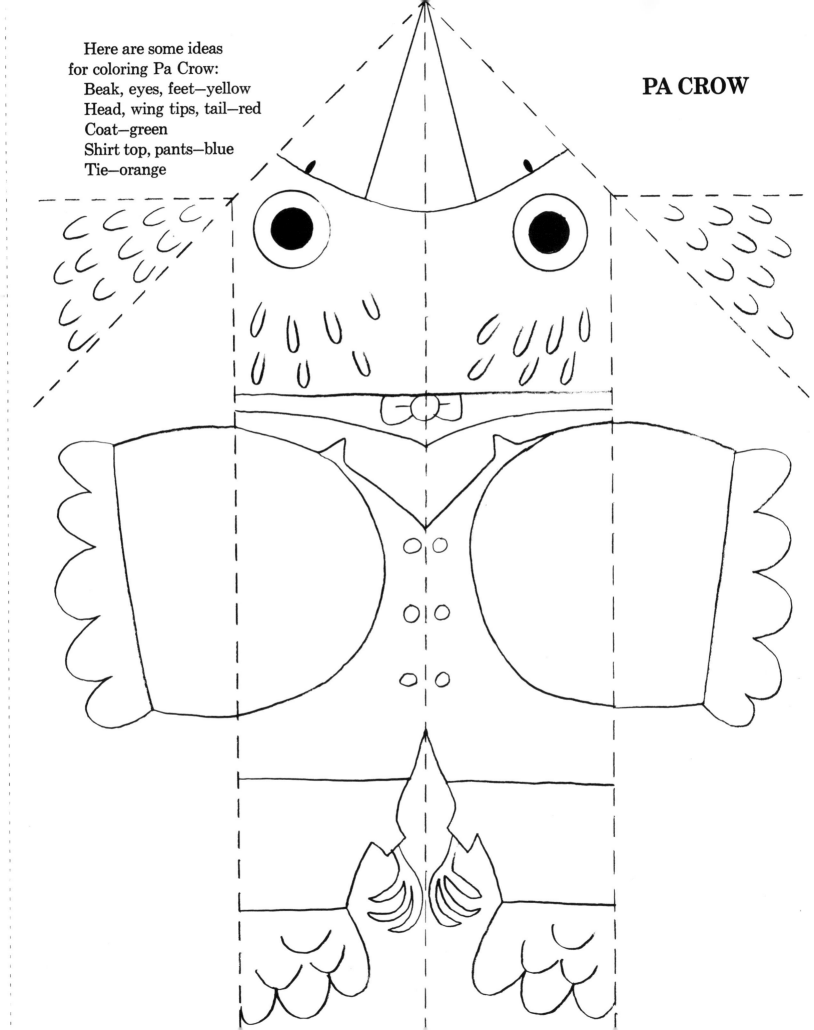

Here are some ideas
for coloring Pa Crow:
Beak, eyes, feet—yellow
Head, wing tips, tail—red
Coat—green
Shirt top, pants—blue
Tie—orange

PA CROW

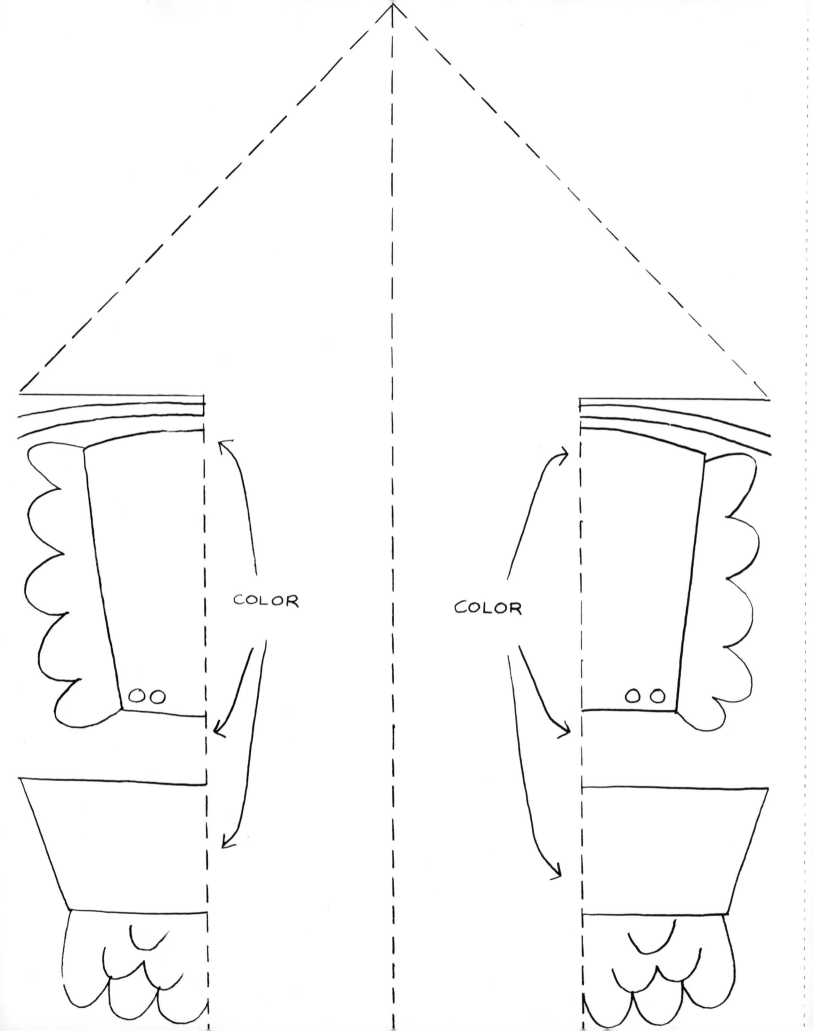

COLOR

COLOR

SOME SPECIAL FRIENDS

Do you know all of these people from Busy Town?
They are saying "hello" to you. Why don't you color
all of them?

Nurse Nelly

Doctor Lion

Stitches

Blacksmith Fox

Daddy Pig

Mommy

Harry

Sally

Mommy Stitches   Abby

Lowly Worm

Wild Bill
Hiccup

Smokey

Sparky

Snozzle

Sawdust,
the carpenter

Bugdozer

Able Baker
Charlie

Zip, the postman

Sergeant Murphy

The pig family is going on vacation. Charlie Dog's taxi can barely hold them all!

balloon

DRINK WATER

blimp

EAT BRUNO'S HOT DOGS

BRUNO'S HOT DOGS

LIFE GUARD

life guard

LIFE GUARD

paper plates

surfer

waves

31 DAYS	AUGUST					
SUNDAY	MONDAY	TUESDAY	WEDNESDAY	THURSDAY	FRIDAY	SATURDAY

Sergeant Murphy rides again!

TICK-TACK-TOE

The players take turns starting the game.

One player uses an "X" mark. The other uses an "O" mark.

They take turns putting their marks in the squares.

Whoever is first to get 3 of his marks in a row is the winner.

Harry Bear just won a game from Tilly Hippo because he got three "O's" in a row.

Would you like to play?

Directions for playing tick-tack-toe are on the other side of the page.

TRANS

Color the drawings on this page and the next 2 pages. Cut them out along the solid black lines. Fold along the dotted lines.

Each car in the train will make a little box. Tuck the side tab inside the box and paste or tape it in place. Then do the same with the roof tab.

Line the cars up and stand the animal cut-outs around them. Have a good trip!

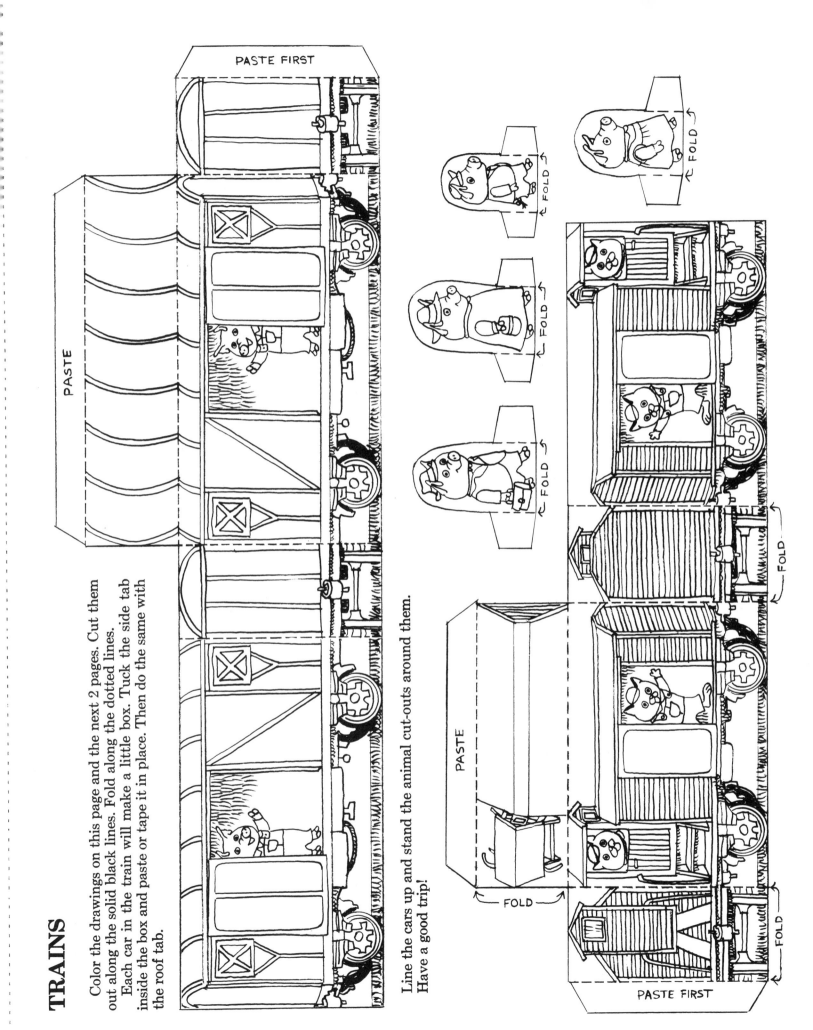

PASTE FIRST

PASTE

FOLD

PASTE

PASTE FIRST

FOLD

Remember—do your cutting on the other side of the page.

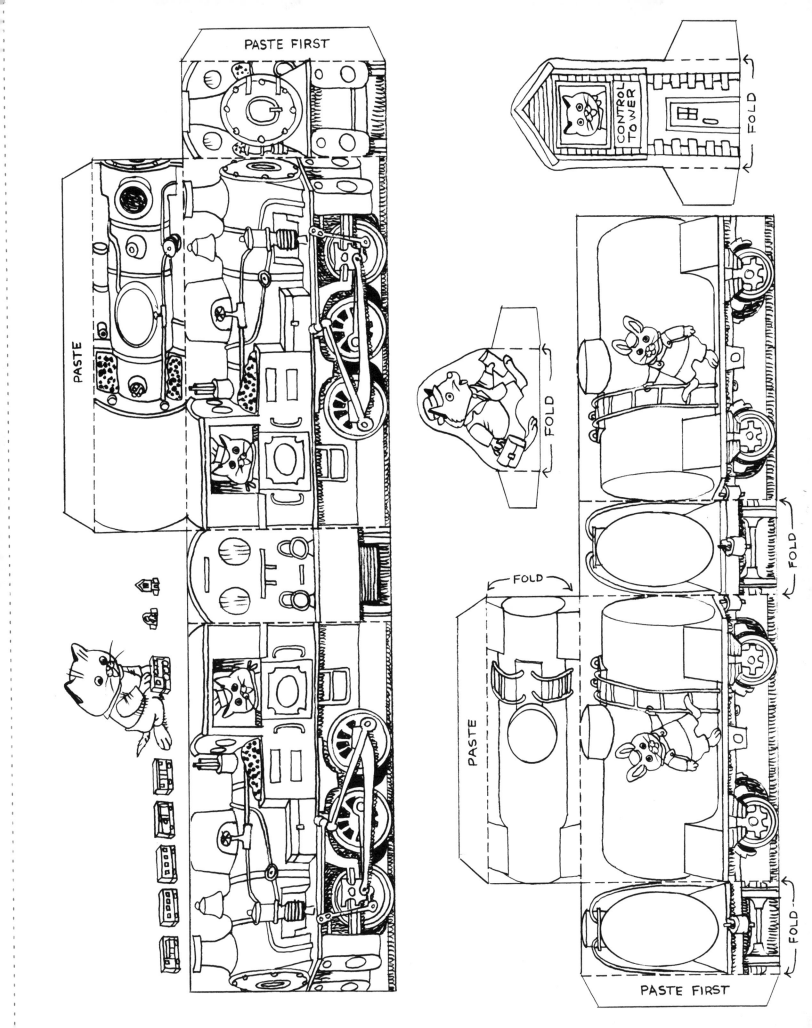

PASTE FIRST

PASTE

CONTROL TOWER

FOLD

FOLD

FOLD

PASTE

FOLD

FOLD

PASTE FIRST

Remember—do your cutting on the other side of the page.

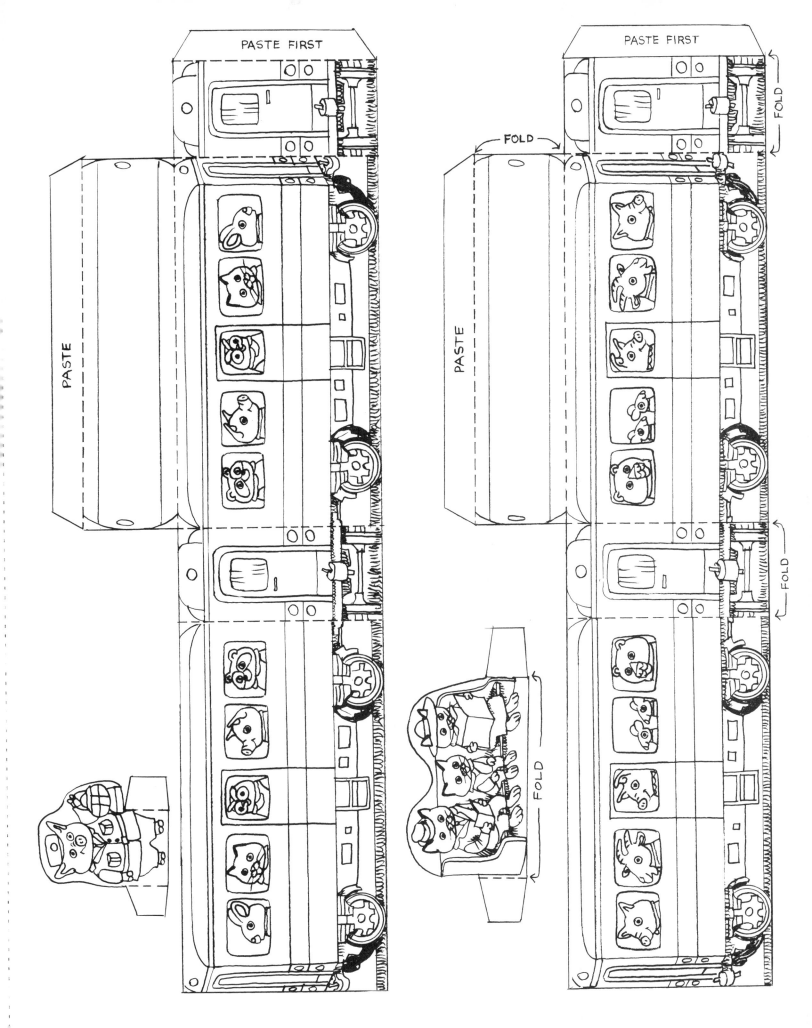

Remember—do your cutting on the other side of the page.

Sam Cat and Dudley Pig are detectives. They dress in many disguises so that no one will know who they are.

Color the turtle and the garbage can—but don't tell anyone who is inside them!

Huckle and Lowly Worm
are off to school.
  When do YOU start school?

30 DAYS	SEPTEMBER				LABOR DAY — 1st MON. IN SEPT.	
SUNDAY	MONDAY	TUESDAY	WEDNESDAY	THURSDAY	FRIDAY	SATURDAY

The fire engine needs a new coat of paint. Will you help paint it?

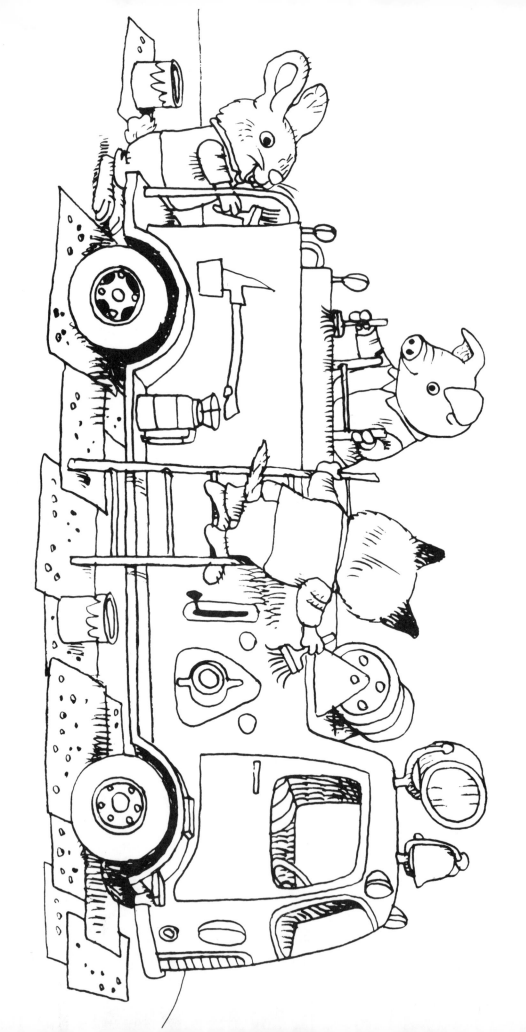

BOOKPLATES

Fill in your name and color the pictures. Cut out along the solid black outlines. Paste onto the inside front cover of your own books.

THIS BOOK BELONGS TO

THIS BOOK BELONGS TO

THIS BOOK BELONGS TO

THIS BOOK BELONGS TO

THIS BOOK BELONGS TO

Remember—do your cutting on the other side of the page.

PASTE

PASTE

PASTE

PASTE

PASTE

BOOKMARKS

Color the pictures, front and back. Cut out, following the solid black outlines on this side of the page. Now you can mark your place when you stop reading.

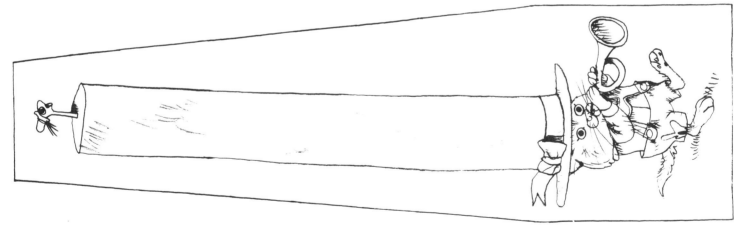

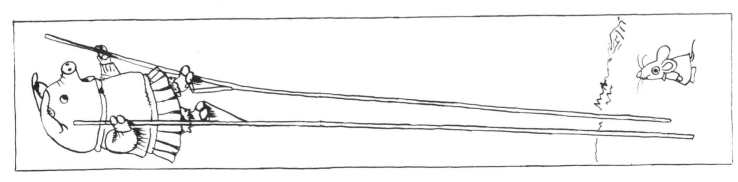

Do your cutting on the other side of the page!

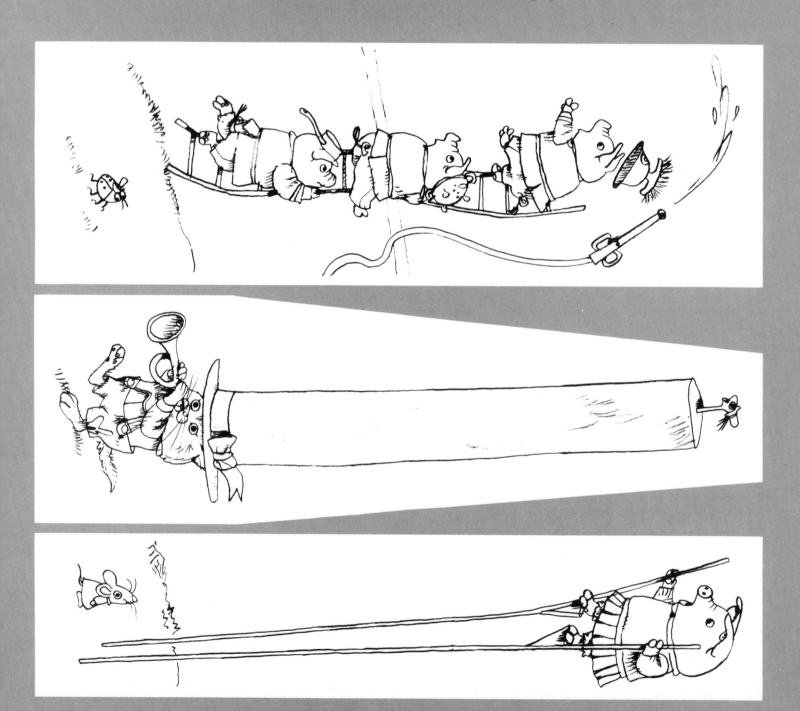

Miss Honey has written the alphabet on the blackboard. Help the children color it in.

Bruno has a picnic.

Count along with Miss Honey and color the numbers.

LEARNING TO COUNT

0 1 2
zero none one two

3 4 5
three four five

6 7
six seven

8 9 10
eight nine ten

2
two

Mr. Pig likes to read stories to Joseph and Josephine.

This is Busy Town.
My, what a nice town!

Huckle has made the world's biggest jack-o'-lantern for Halloween.

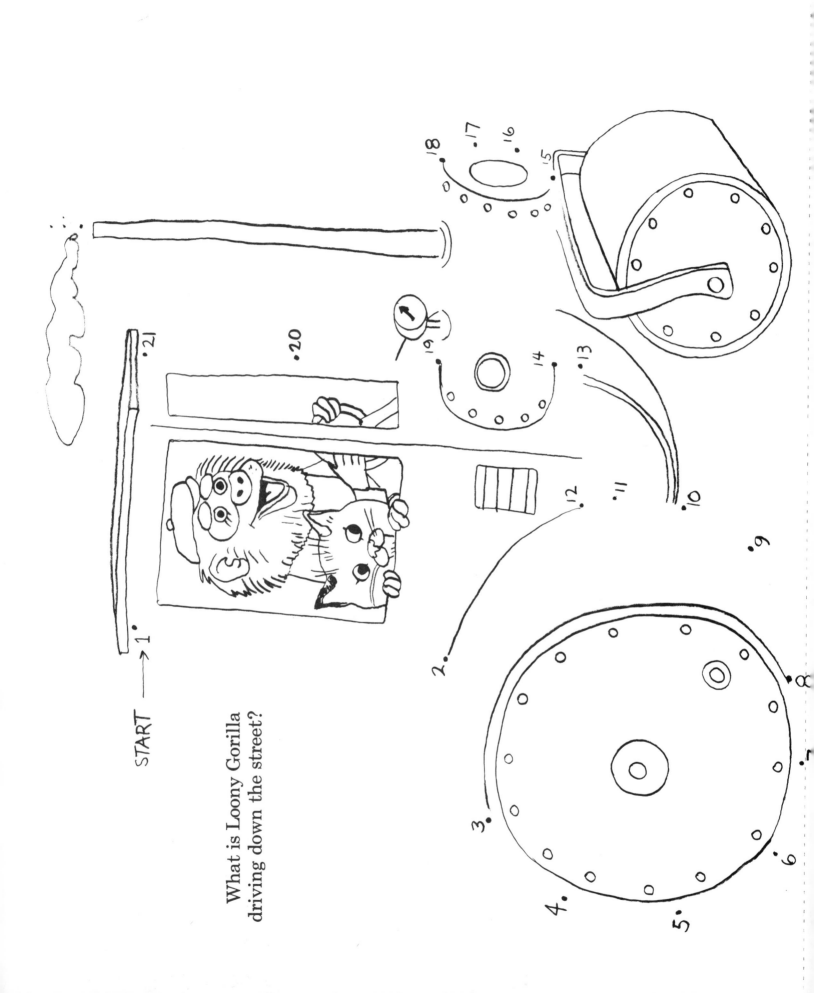

START →

What is Loony Gorilla driving down the street?

OCTOBER

31 DAYS · HALLOWEEN—OCT. 31

SUNDAY	MONDAY	TUESDAY	WEDNESDAY	THURSDAY	FRIDAY	SATURDAY

APPLES

apple cider

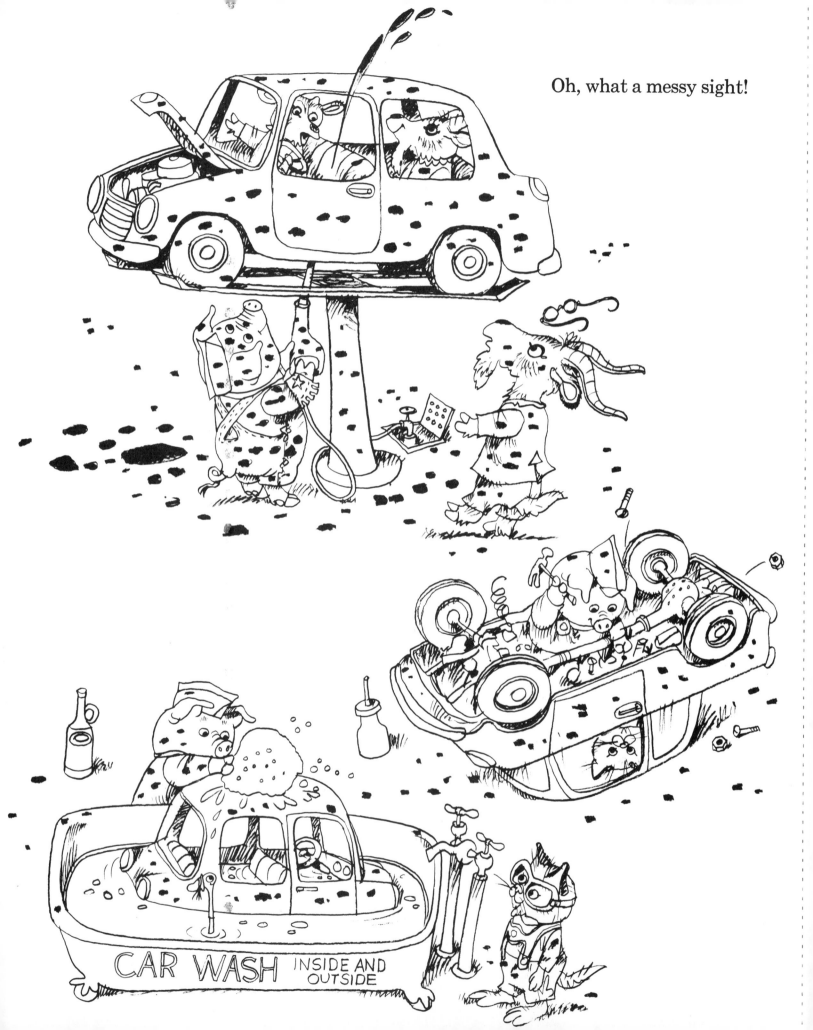

Oh, what a messy sight!

Who wants to play?

Time for a checkup. Say "Aah!"

Look at all the different drivers in Busy Town!

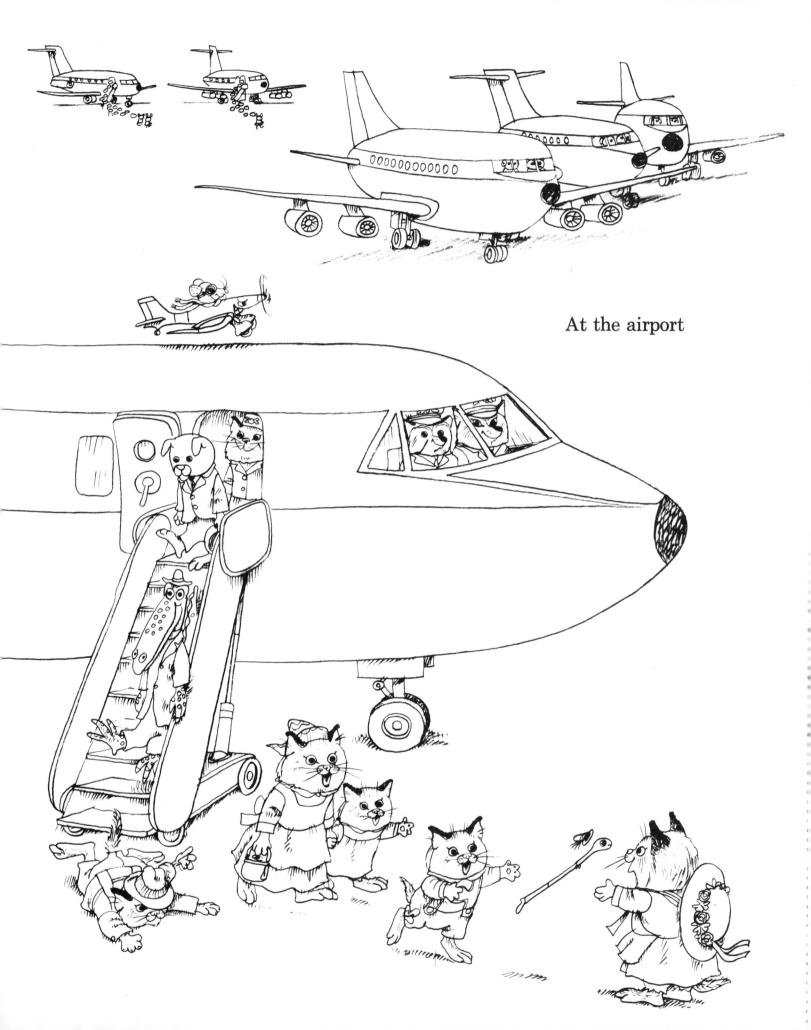

At the airport

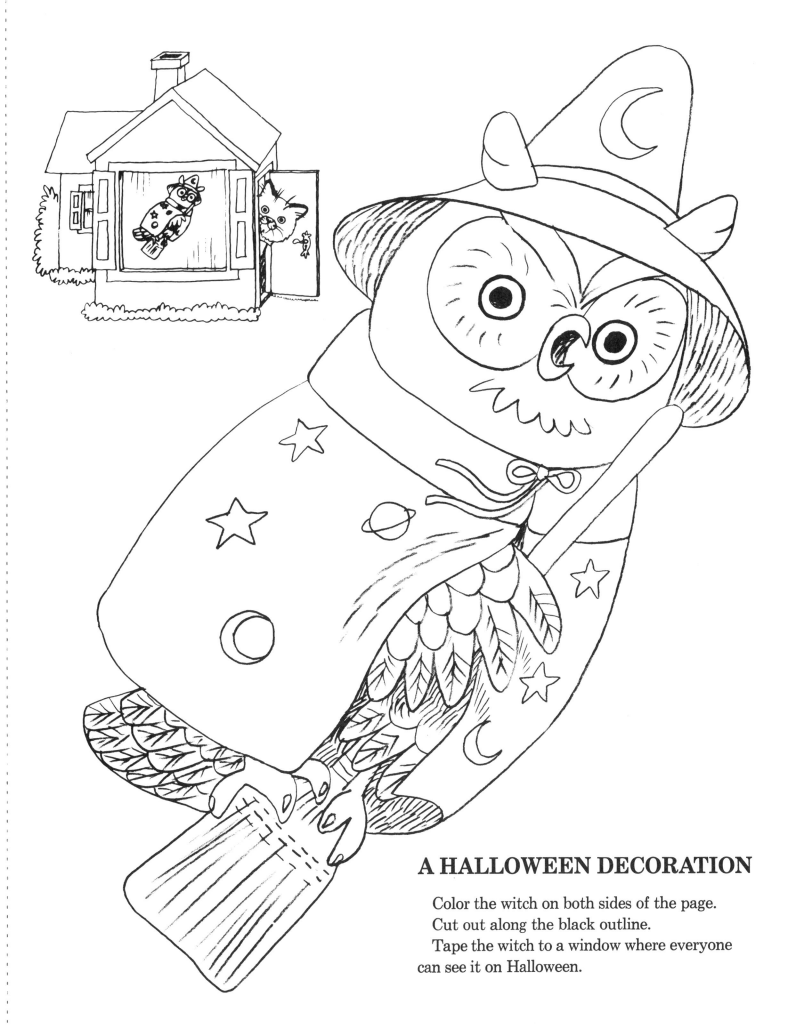

A HALLOWEEN DECORATION

Color the witch on both sides of the page.
Cut out along the black outline.
Tape the witch to a window where everyone
can see it on Halloween.

Mr. Skunk is digging the
cellar for a new house.

Mr. Puffin and
Mr. Parrot are
going to a party.
My, they look
nice in their good
clothes!

NOVEMBER

30 DAYS

THANKSGIVING DAY—
4th THURSDAY IN NOV.

SUNDAY	MONDAY	TUESDAY	WEDNESDAY	THURSDAY	FRIDAY	SATURDAY

The good ship IRISH PENNANT is finally starting her cruise. Did you see everyone getting ready earlier?

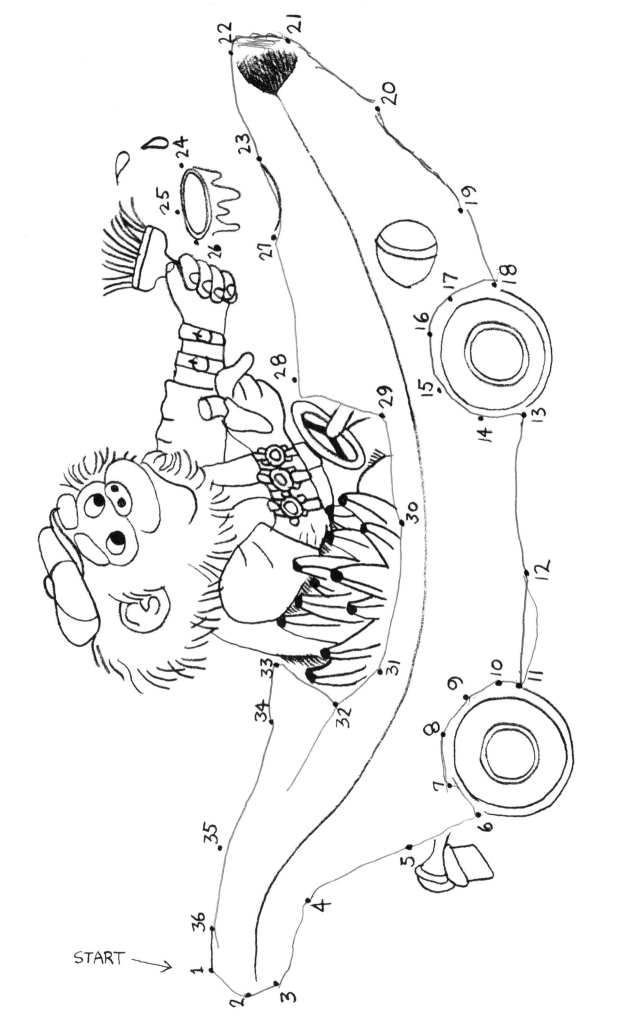

START →

What is Bananas Gorilla painting? Connect the dots and find out.

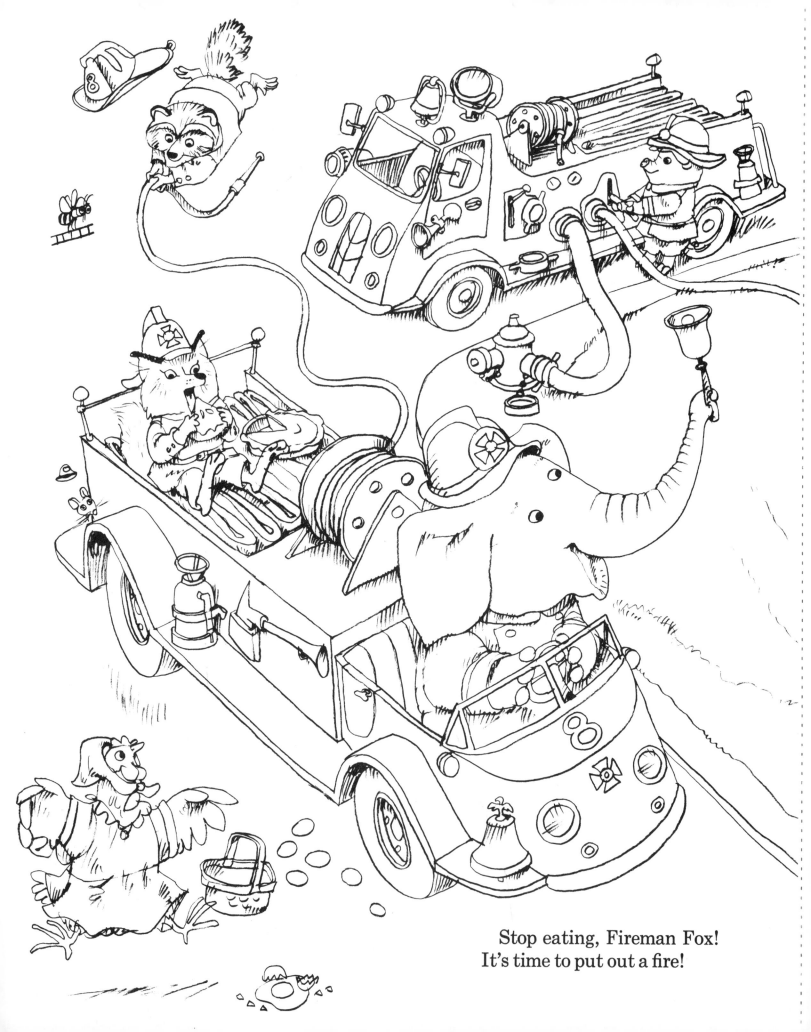

Stop eating, Fireman Fox!
It's time to put out a fire!

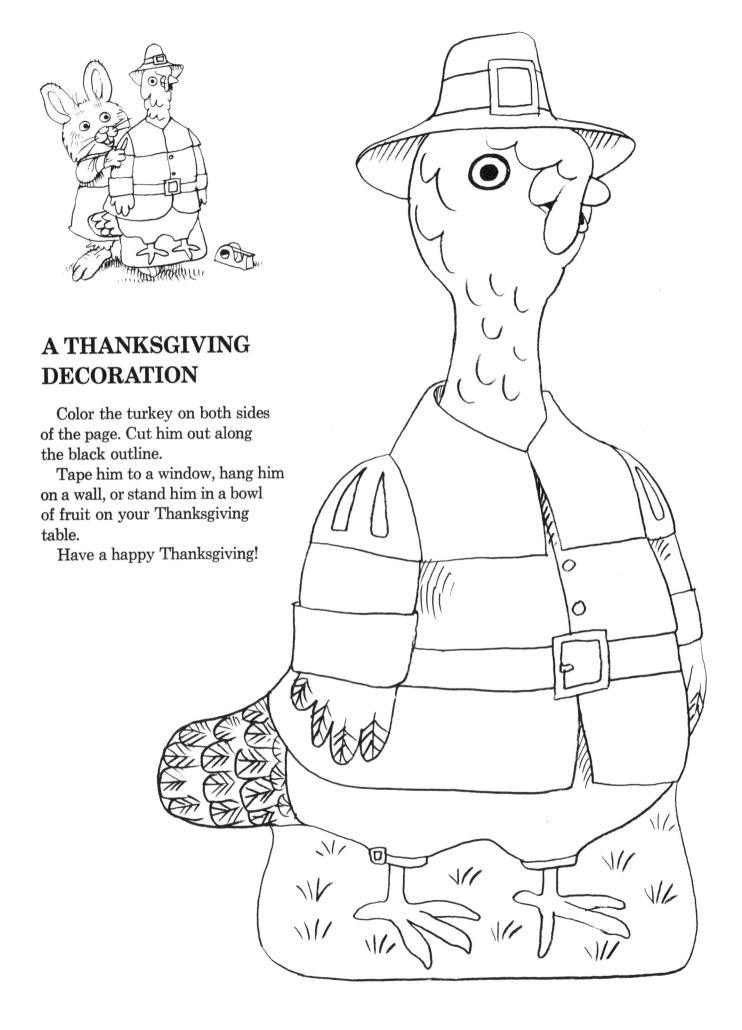

A THANKSGIVING DECORATION

Color the turkey on both sides of the page. Cut him out along the black outline.

Tape him to a window, hang him on a wall, or stand him in a bowl of fruit on your Thanksgiving table.

Have a happy Thanksgiving!

Oh-oh! Guess what's going to happen next!

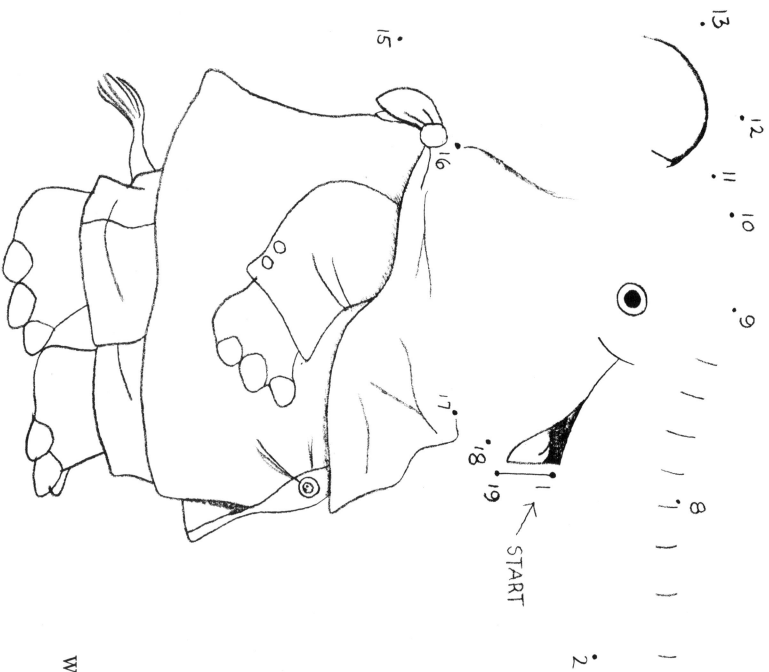

Who could this be?

31 DAYS		DECEMBER		CHRISTMAS DAY — DECEMBER 25		
SUNDAY	MONDAY	TUESDAY	WEDNESDAY	THURSDAY	FRIDAY	SATURDAY

A quiet corner in Busy Town

How to make
"MR. PAINT PIG PAINTS THINGS"
A book colored by you

1. On the next four pages are little pages for your book. Follow the instructions on each little page and color what they tell you to. Then color the other things in the picture, too!

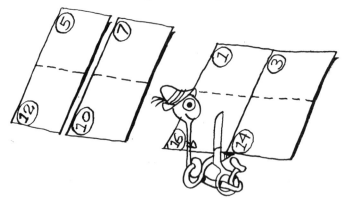

2. Tear the sheets of little pages out of this book. Cut each sheet apart along the solid black line.

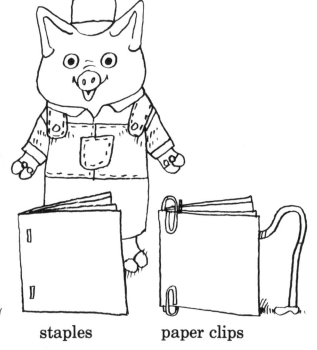

3. You now have four sheets of little pages. Fold each sheet along the dotted line. The numbers on the pages should match the order of the numbers in the picture above.

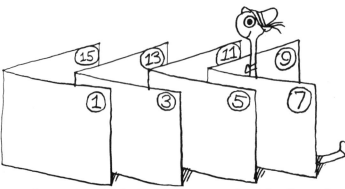

4. Place the folded sheets, one inside the other, in the order of the page numbers shown above.

5. Hold the pages all together with:

string or notebook rings, through punched holes

a large rubber band

a string or ribbon

staples

paper clips

Now you have made your very own book about Mr. Paint Pig!

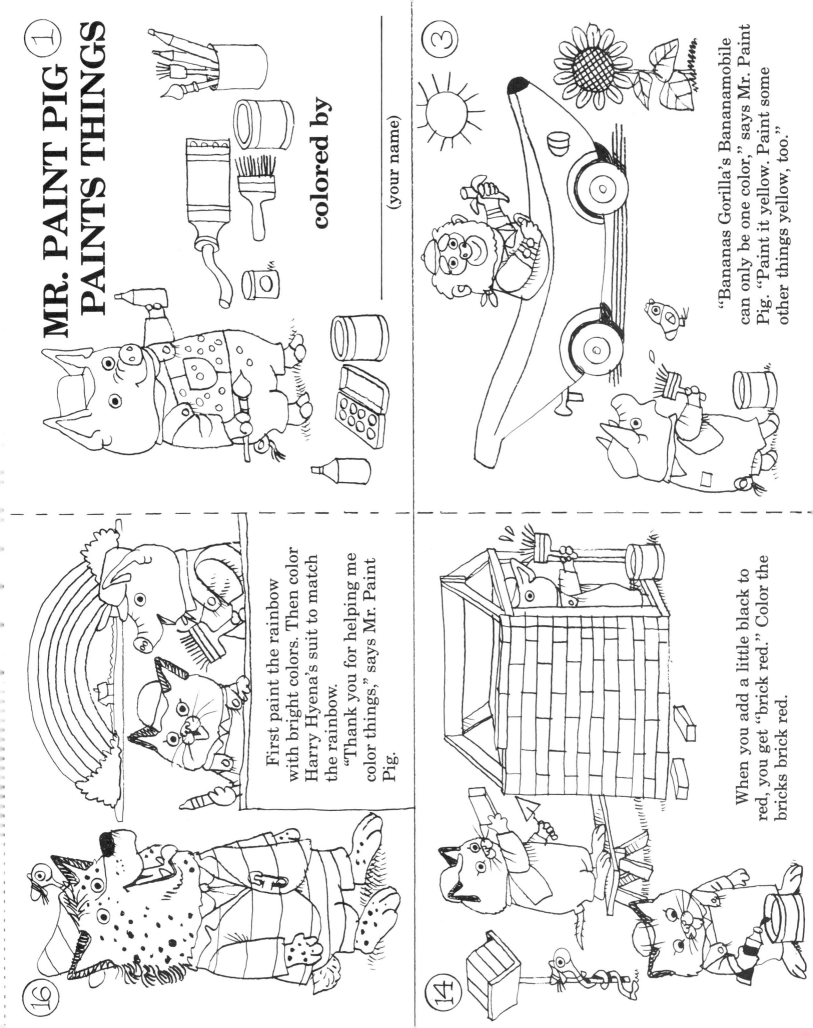

MR. PAINT PIG PAINTS THINGS

(1)

colored by

_____
(your name)

(3)

"Bananas Gorilla's Bananamobile can only be one color," says Mr. Paint Pig. "Paint it yellow. Paint some other things yellow, too."

(16)

First paint the rainbow with bright colors. Then color Harry Hyena's suit to match the rainbow.

"Thank you for helping me color things," says Mr. Paint Pig.

(14)

When you add a little black to red, you get "brick red." Color the bricks brick red.

④

Paint Ms. Mouse's house blue. Be careful you don't spill the paint!

②

Mr. Paint Pig and Huckle Cat have many things to paint today. Will you help them?
"Please paint that fire engine red," says Mr. Paint Pig.

⑮

When you add a little black to green, you get "pickle green." Color the pickle car pickle green.

⑬

Mr. Frumble bought a hot dog with mustard. Some of the mustard got on his face and clothes while he was eating it. Paint the hot dog red and the mustard yellow, and paint some mustard spots on Mr. Frumble.

MUSTARD

HOT DOGS

⑤

When you mix red and yellow together, they make orange. Paint the train orange with red wheels.

⑦

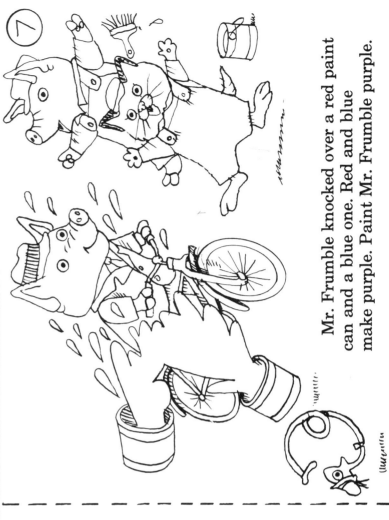

Mr. Frumble knocked over a red paint can and a blue one. Red and blue make purple. Paint Mr. Frumble purple.

⑫

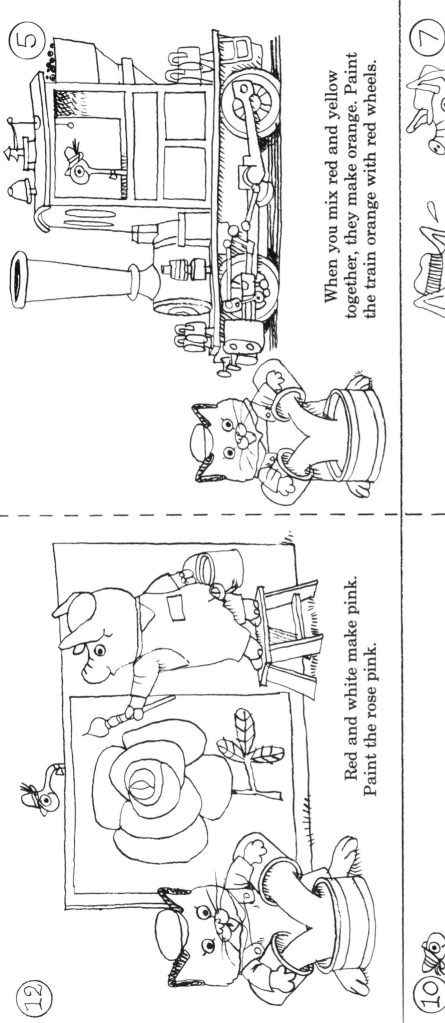

Red and white make pink. Paint the rose pink.

⑩

Draw a white snowman. Give him black eyes, a black mouth, and a black hat. Make his nose with an orange carrot.

COAL

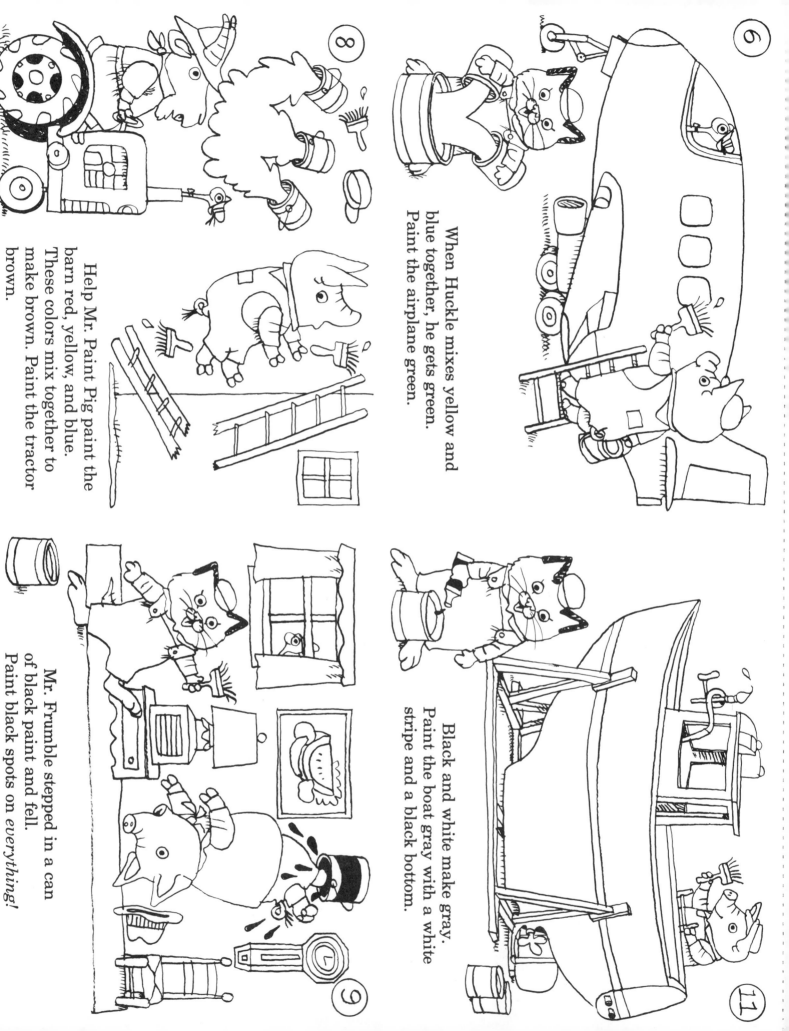

8

Help Mr. Paint Pig paint the barn red, yellow, and blue. These colors mix together to make brown. Paint the tractor brown.

9

When Huckle mixes yellow and blue together, he gets green. Paint the airplane green.

6

Mr. Frumble stepped in a can of black paint and fell. Paint black spots on *everything!*

11

Black and white make gray. Paint the boat gray with a white stripe and a black bottom.

Mr. Paint Pig says,
"Here is a picture of
Sergeant Murphy for
you to color.
Be sure to color his
motorcycle red!"

GAMES TO MAKE AND PLAY

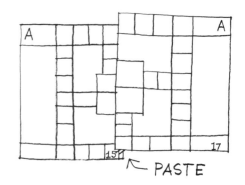

How to make the games:

Color the markers and "dice" on the next page. The "dice" should be red with black dots. Cut out the markers and "dice" following the solid black outlines. Fold markers along the dotted lines. Tuck the tab of each marker inside and paste or tape in place, as the picture on the page shows.

On the two pages following the one with the markers, use one color to fill every other square of the game board. Now fill the squares in between with a different color. Tear the two pages out. Paste the second page to the first as the picture at right shows. This will give you the game "board" for Game A. Game B will be on the back side of Game A.

Rules for Game A:
HURRY ON HOME!
YOUR MOTHER'S
CALLING YOU!

1. To start, each player (Bunny, Fox, Cat, Pig) stands at his or her own "start" box.

2. Beginning with the Bunny and going clockwise around the game board, the players take turns dropping the paper "dice." A player cannot enter the game until he or she gets a 3 or 4 on the dice. Then he can move around the board. (See "How to move" below.)

3. Moving clockwise, each player goes around 3½ sides of the game board to reach his "house" and find out what his mother is calling him for.

4. If two players land on the same space, the player who was on the space first must go back 2 spaces and lose 1 turn.

5. Some spaces contain rewards and penalties. Players must follow the instructions on these spaces when they land on them.

6. The first player to arrive at his or her house wins the game. The other players continue playing until they, too, arrive home.

Rules for Game B:
HURRY, FIREFIGHTERS!
PUT OUT THAT FIRE!

1. All firefighters (players) start in the firehouse.

2. Each player drops the paper "dice." The person with the highest number goes first, the next highest goes second, etc.

3. The players move along the road to the fire by dropping the dice in turn. (See "How to move" below.)

4. More than one player may be on the same space at a time.

5. Some spaces contain rewards and penalties. Players must follow the instructions on these spaces when they land on them.

6. The firefighter who first gets to the fire puts it out and wins the game. The game is then over.

How to move:

Hold the paper "dice" in your hand. Let them fall to the floor. Count how many dots are facing up. Move that number of spaces.

Help me count the dots, Lowly!

☐	☐	☐	Lose your turn
⚀	☐	☐	Move 1 space
⚀	⚀	☐	Move 2 spaces
⚁	☐	☐	Move 2 spaces
⚀	⚁	☐	Move 3 spaces

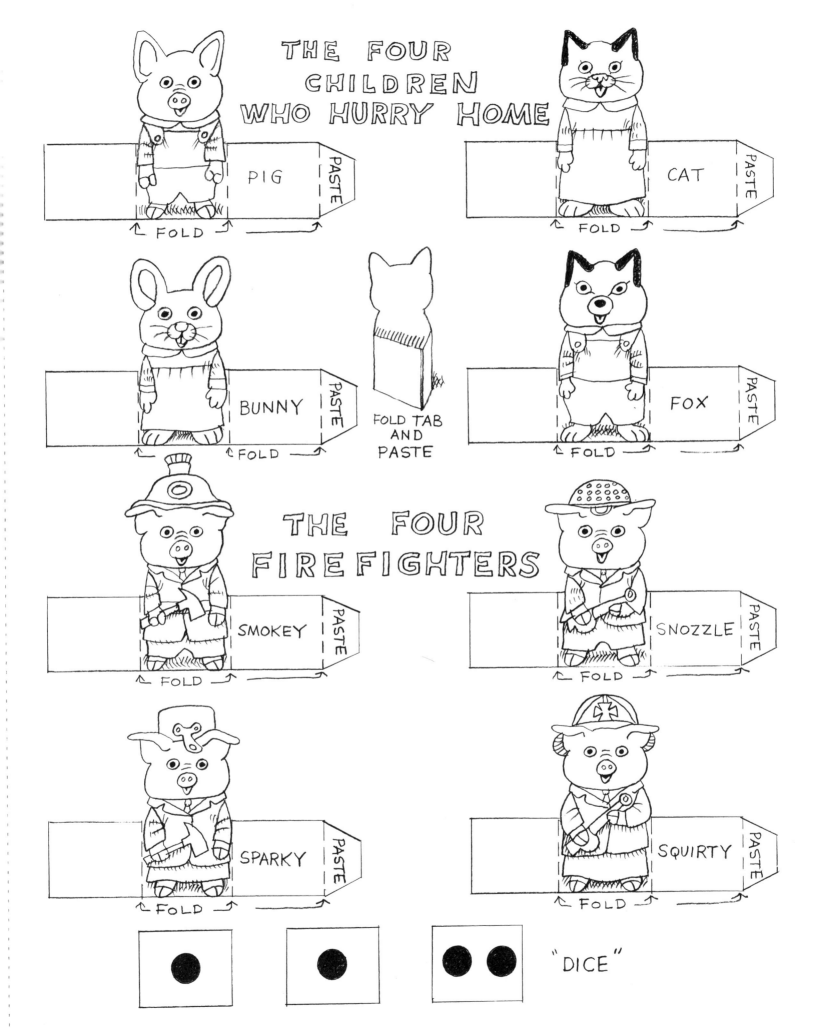

THE FOUR CHILDREN WHO HURRY HOME

PIG PASTE FOLD

CAT PASTE FOLD

BUNNY PASTE FOLD

FOLD TAB AND PASTE

FOX PASTE FOLD

THE FOUR FIREFIGHTERS

SMOKEY PASTE FOLD

SNOZZLE PASTE FOLD

SPARKY PASTE FOLD

SQUIRTY PASTE FOLD

"DICE"

START

GAME A

TAKE A
DEEP BREATH
GO AHEAD 1

GET STUCK
ON FENCE
GO BACK 3

TRIP OVER
ROCK
LOSE 1 TURN

CAT'S
HOUSE

HURRY
ON
HOME!
YOUR
MOTHER'S
CALLING
You!

FALL IN MUD
PUDDLE
GO BACK 3

FOX'S
HOUSE

RUN
DOWNHILL
GO AHEAD 1

← PASTE OTHER PART OF GAME HERE

START

TIE YOUR
SHOELACE
LOSE 1 TURN

Mr. Paint Pig says,
"Lowly Worm and Huckle Cat
are taking a walk. Will you
please color them and draw
some grass under their feet?"

HALLOWEEN MASKS

Halloween is the time when we put on masks and go out into the night to frighten people. Color in this spooky Halloween tale.

Bunny Rabbit has made a fierce fox mask and is all set to go out and frighten somebody.

Billy Goat has made a scary owl mask. Whom will he frighten tonight?

Bunny and Billy meet in the dark night. When they see each other, they are both so scared that they run right home.

Bunny telephones Billy.
"Did you see what I saw tonight?" he says.
"I saw a scary owl with HORNS!"
"You should have seen what I saw!" says Billy.
"I saw a fierce fox with long EARS! Boy! Was I scared!"

So, when you wear YOUR mask, try to hide your long ears and horns so you won't frighten people too much! You can make your own mask with cut-outs from pages 25 and 27.

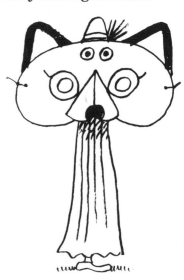

It's a good thing that Billy and Bunny didn't run into Lowly wearing his mask. He is the most frightening thing ever!

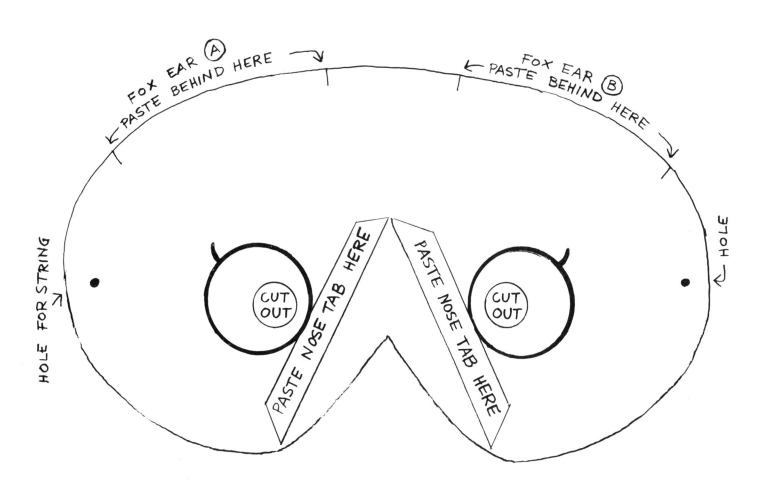

Directions for making Halloween masks are on the next page.

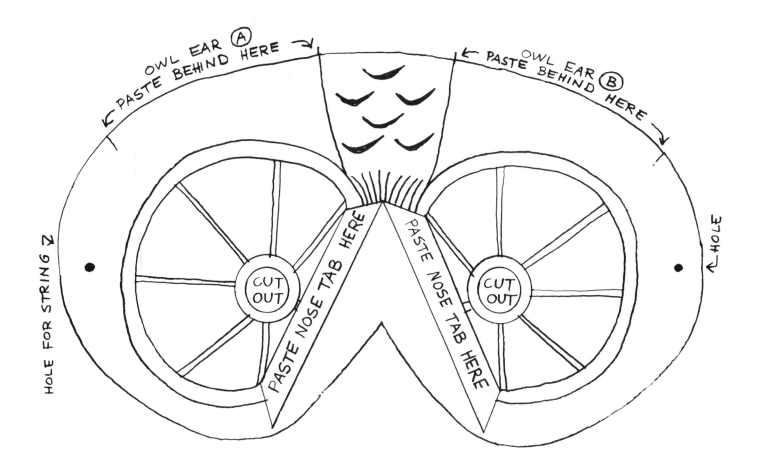

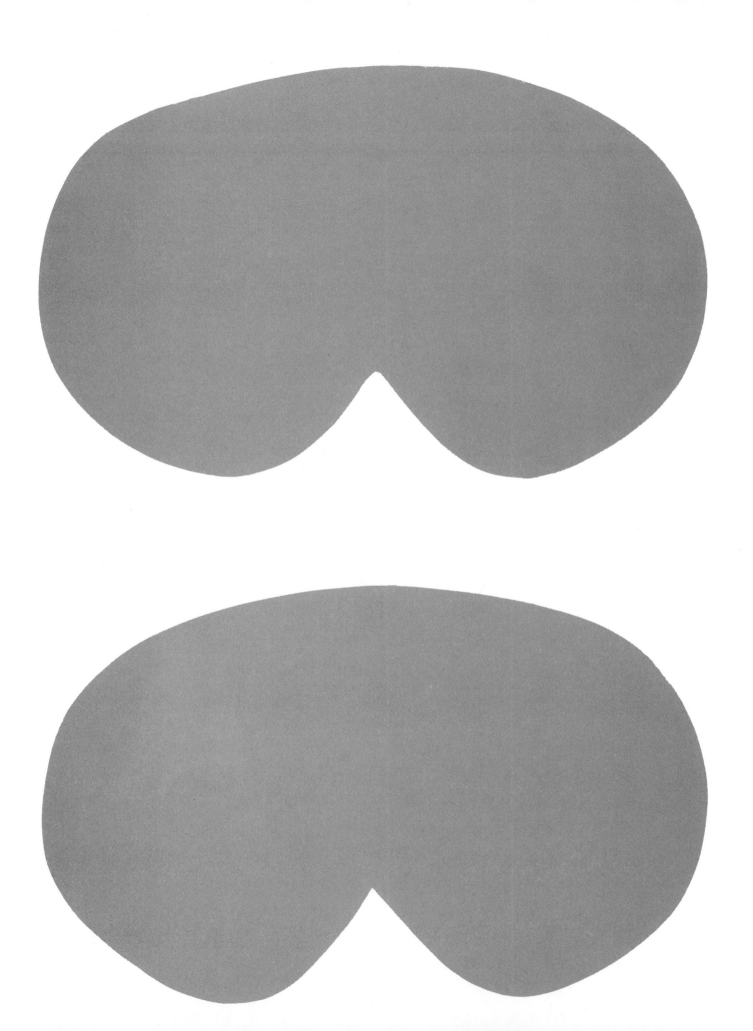

Color the pieces on this page and the page before it. Yellow is a good color for Owl's beak and eyes. Try using different colors for the different pieces of the masks. Cut out the pieces. Gently fold each mask to cut out the eyeholes. Paste on the ears and nose. Fasten strings through holes in the sides of the mask and tie them together at the back of your head.

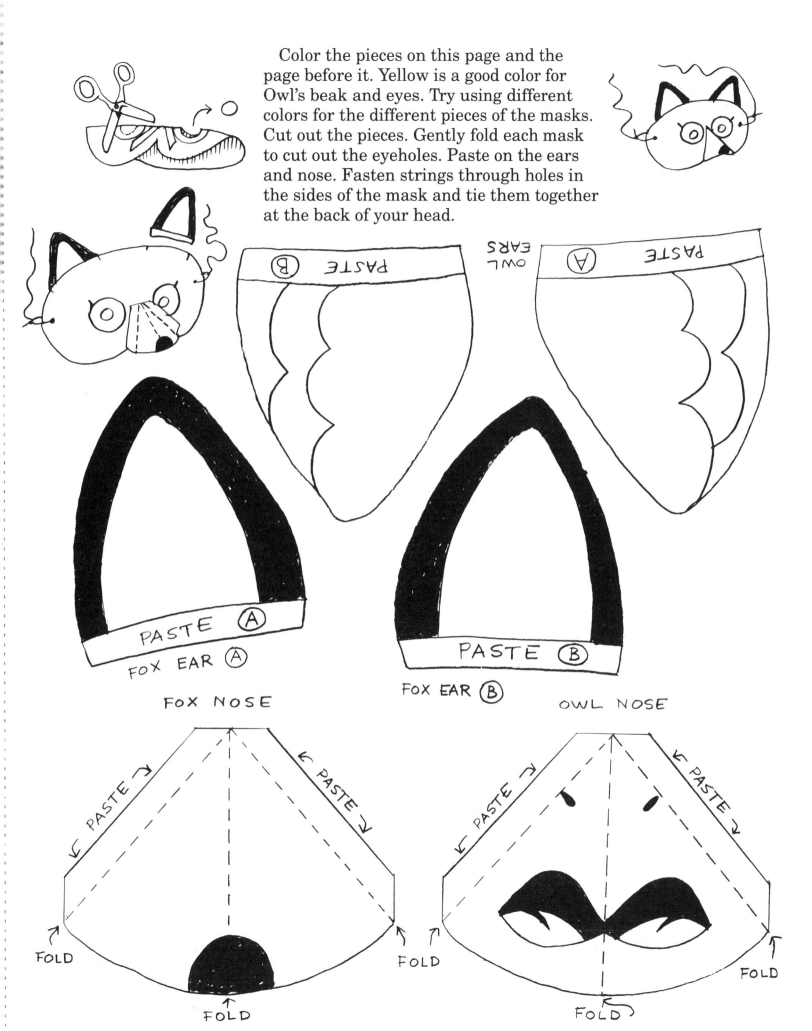

PASTE Ⓑ

PASTE
OWL
EARS

PASTE Ⓐ

PASTE Ⓐ

FOX EAR Ⓐ

PASTE Ⓑ

FOX EAR Ⓑ

FOX NOSE

OWL NOSE

PASTE

PASTE

FOLD

FOLD

FOLD

PASTE

PASTE

FOLD

FOLD

FOLD

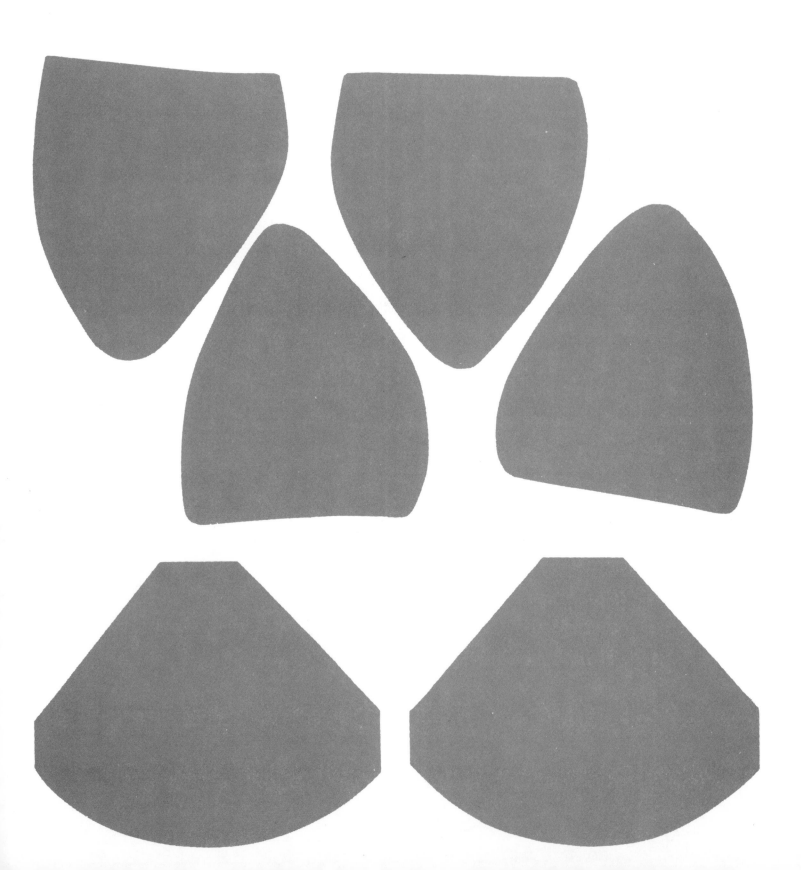

Mr. Paint Pig says,
"Big Tilly loves ice cream.
Give her a pink ice-cream cone
with chocolate sprinkles."

How to make "MY LOWLY WORM BOOK"

with drawings by you

1. On the next four pages are little pages for your book. Follow the instructions on each little page and draw what they tell you to. Color the pictures.

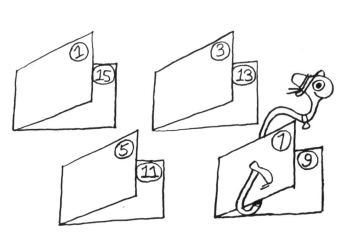

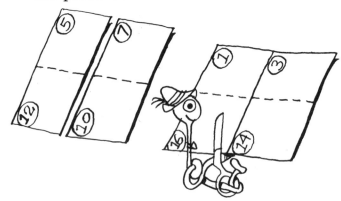

2. Tear the sheets of little pages out of this book. Cut each sheet apart along the solid black line.

3. You now have four sheets of little pages. Fold each sheet along the dotted line. The numbers on the pages should match the order of the numbers in the picture above.

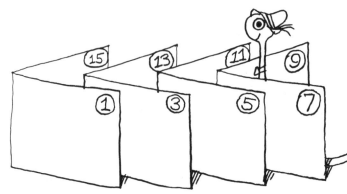

4. Place the folded sheets, one inside the other, in the order of the page numbers shown above.

5. Hold the pages all together with:

string or notebook rings, through punched holes

a large rubber band

a string or ribbon

staples

paper clips

Now you have made your very own MY LOWLY WORM BOOK!

MY LOWLY WORM BOOK

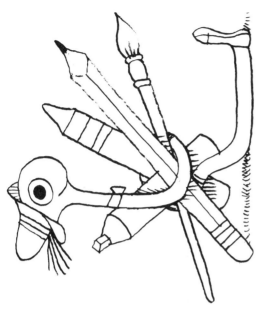

with drawings and coloring by

_____
(your name)

He ate a fried egg and peas for breakfast.
(Draw a fried egg on his plate. Draw some
peas on his spoon. A whole lot of peas!)

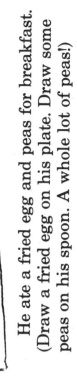

Lowly got home safely.
He put on his napkin and
ate his supper.
(Draw Lowly eating his supper.)
Does it taste good, Lowly?

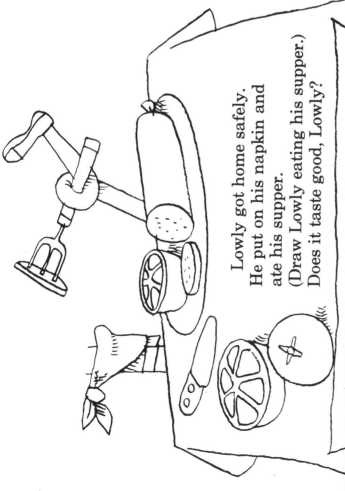

Lowly got into his car to drive home.
(Draw some other cars in the parking lot. Color
a pink car, a green car, and an orange car.)

2 Lowly Worm looked in the refrigerator to find something to eat for breakfast. (Draw some milk and eggs and fruit and vegetables in the refrigerator.)

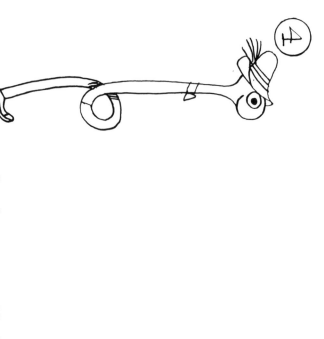

4 Lowly went outside. The sun was shining brightly. (Draw the sun. Draw a tree and a house.)

15 But he backed into a street cleaner's wagon. (Draw a broom in the street cleaner's hands so he can clean up the mess.)

13 Lowly paid for the food he wanted. (Color in his groceries. Draw some pennies and dimes and dollar bills on the check-out counter.)

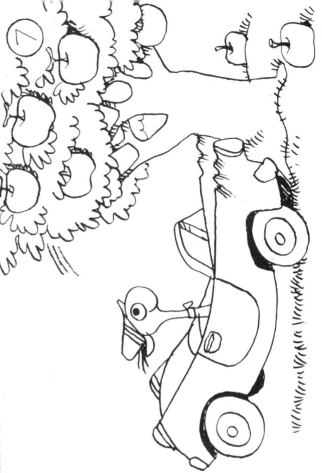

(5)

He got into his car to go for a ride.
(Draw wheels on his car so that it can go.
What color is Lowly's car?)

(7)

Then he bumped into an apple tree.
(Draw an apple falling on Lowly's head.)

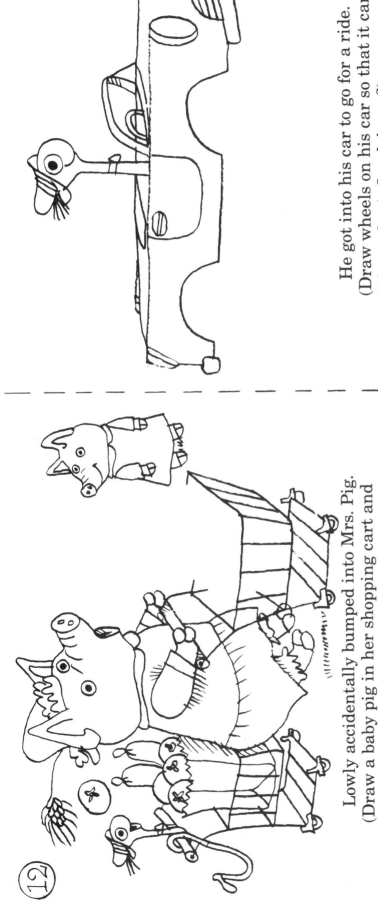

(12)

Lowly accidentally bumped into Mrs. Pig.
(Draw a baby pig in her shopping cart and
color her dress purple.)

(10)

Lowly went into the market and bought some hot dogs.
(Draw some hot dogs on the butcher's cutting block.)

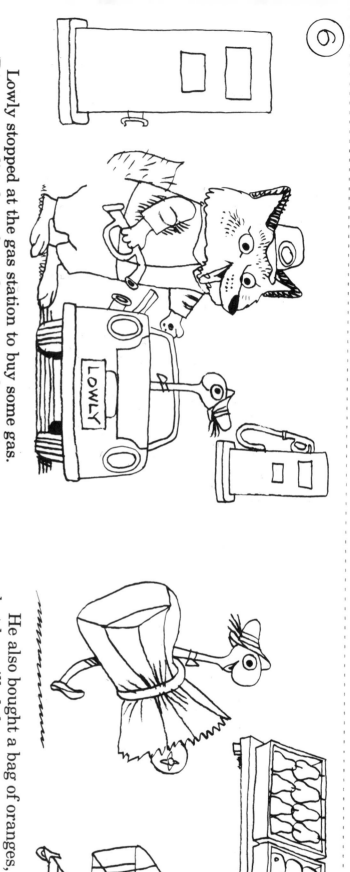

6

Lowly stopped at the gas station to buy some gas. (Draw a gasoline hose from the pump to the nozzle and fill up Lowly's gas tank.)

He also bought a bag of oranges, but he spilled them. (Draw some oranges spilling out of the bag. Color in the other fruit, too.)

11

8

Lowly ate the apple while Fixit Cat fixed his car. (Draw a hammer in Fixit's hand. Then color the car hood red.)

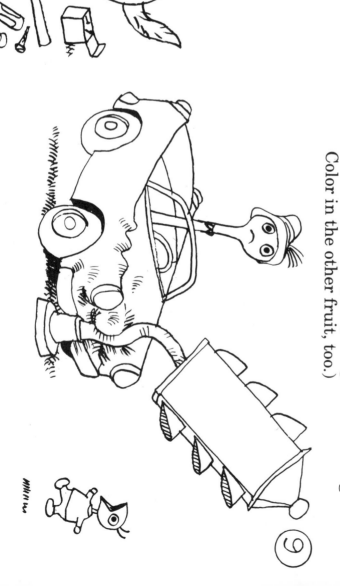

9

BUSYTOWN

Busytown is a very busy place. Here are some of the people who live there. Let's see what they do. You can use as many colors as you like here.

Police Officer Sally stops the traffic to let Big Tilly cross the street.
Oh, Mr. Frumble! That's not the way to stop!

Sergeant Murphy chases after speeding apples and bananas.

Some people are busy sleepers.

Bugdozer repairs the streets.

Nurse Nelly is borrowing a book
from the library. Why don't you
borrow a book or two?

LIBRARY

DRIVE-IN BANK

TOOTHPASTE

Dr. Dentist drives into the drive-in bank
to get some money from Minnie Pig.
We need money to do our shopping.
Let's get some, too.

FISH MARKET

TAXI

Tom, the taxi driver, drives
people all around Busytown.

Mayor Fox inspects
the town to see that
everyone is doing his
or her job.

Hello,
there!

Shall we have fish for supper?
Let's buy some fish at the fish market.

GROCERIES

Grocer Cat fills Ma Pig's bag
with groceries. Fill up your bag
with groceries.

Slice, the butcher, slices
baloney for Little Sister.
Let's buy some baloney.

Trucks are always busy
in Busytown.

GAS AND OIL

AIR

Mr. Stamp, the postman, has his
gas tank filled at the gas station.

Huckle puts air in his tires.

Now you can make your own Busytown by first coloring and then cutting out the buildings, cars, and people on the next few pages. Cut along the solid black lines. Fold along the dotted lines.

FOLD TOWARD YOU

This is how to fold your buildings so that they stand up.

FOLD AWAY FROM YOU

This is how to fold and paste your cars and people. Tuck the tab inside when you paste.

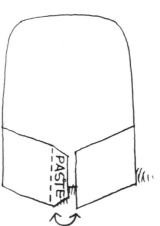

PASTE TOGETHER

Are you all set?

PASTE TOGETHER

LET'S GO!

FOLD

FOLD

PASTE

POST OFFICE

FLOWERS

TOYS

Directions for making Busytown are on the facing page.

PASTE

FOLD

TOWN HALL

WATCH REPAIR

POLICE

NEWS

FOLD

FOLD FOLD FOLD

LIBRARY

DRIVE-IN BANK

FISH MARKET

← CUT OUT →

DEPOSIT AND WITHDRAW MONEY HERE

Books to cut out and borrow from the library

You can deposit this money at the bank. You can withdraw it, too!

Fish to buy at the fish market

1 2
5 10
20 50
100

FOLD FOLD

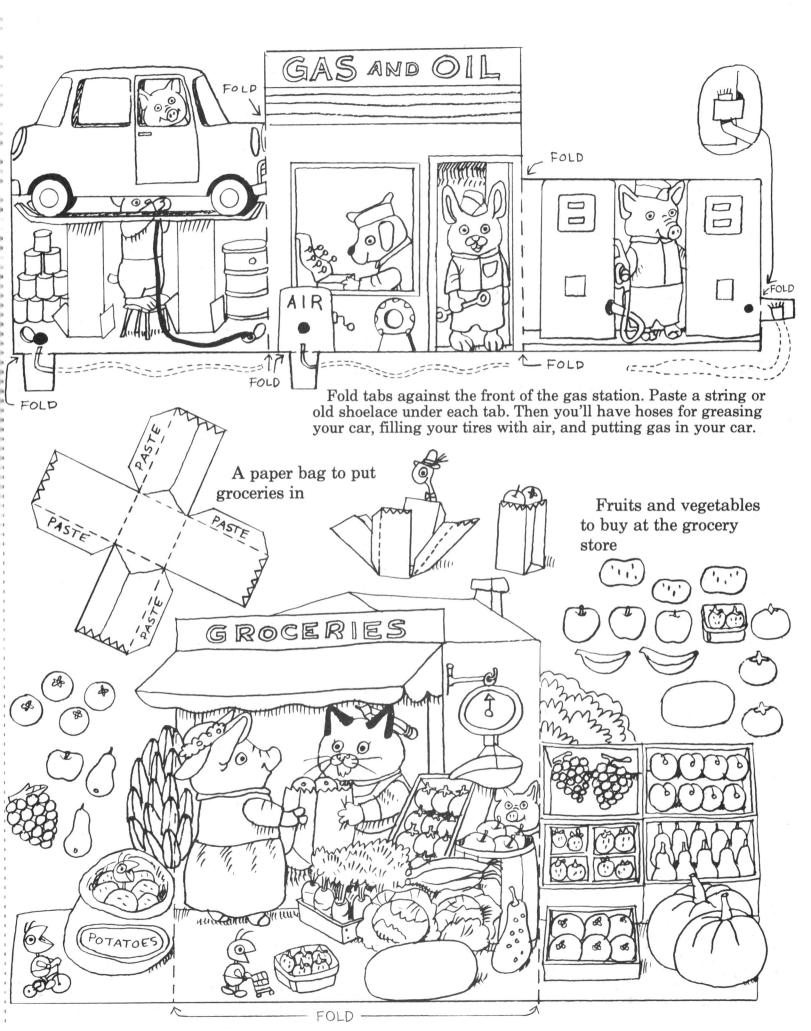

GAS AND OIL

FOLD

FOLD

FOLD

AIR

FOLD

FOLD

FOLD

FOLD

Fold tabs against the front of the gas station. Paste a string or old shoelace under each tab. Then you'll have hoses for greasing your car, filling your tires with air, and putting gas in your car.

PASTE

PASTE

PASTE

PASTE

A paper bag to put groceries in

Fruits and vegetables to buy at the grocery store

GROCERIES

POTATOES

FOLD

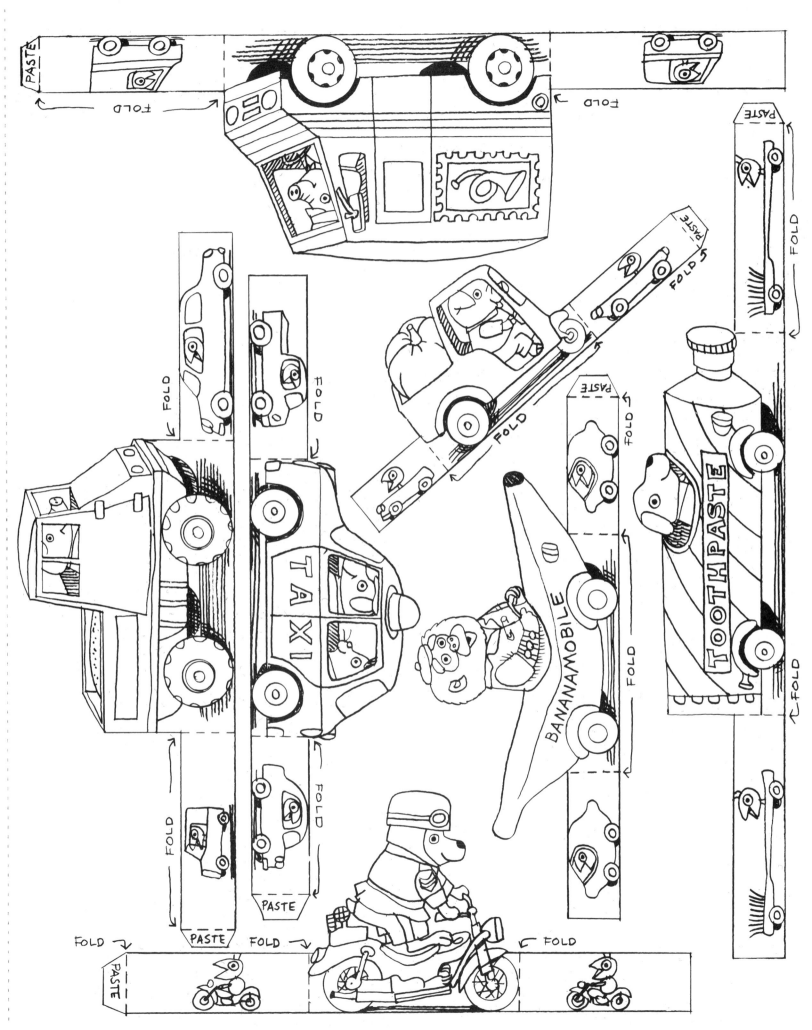

BUGDOZER

PASTE — FOLD

LOWLY WORM

FOLD

PASTE

LITTLE SISTER

FOLD

PASTE

HUCKLE

FOLD

PASTE

STOP

PASTE

DR. LION

FOLD

DR. LION

POLICE OFFICER SALLY

FOLD

PASTE

BIG TILLY

PASTE

FOLD

NURSE NELLY

FOLD

PASTE

MAYOR FOX

FOLD

PASTE

Baloney to buy from Slice, the butcher

MR. FRUMBLE

FOLD

SLICE THE BUTCHER

FOLD

PASTE

LOWLY WORM LEARNS HOW TO GROW

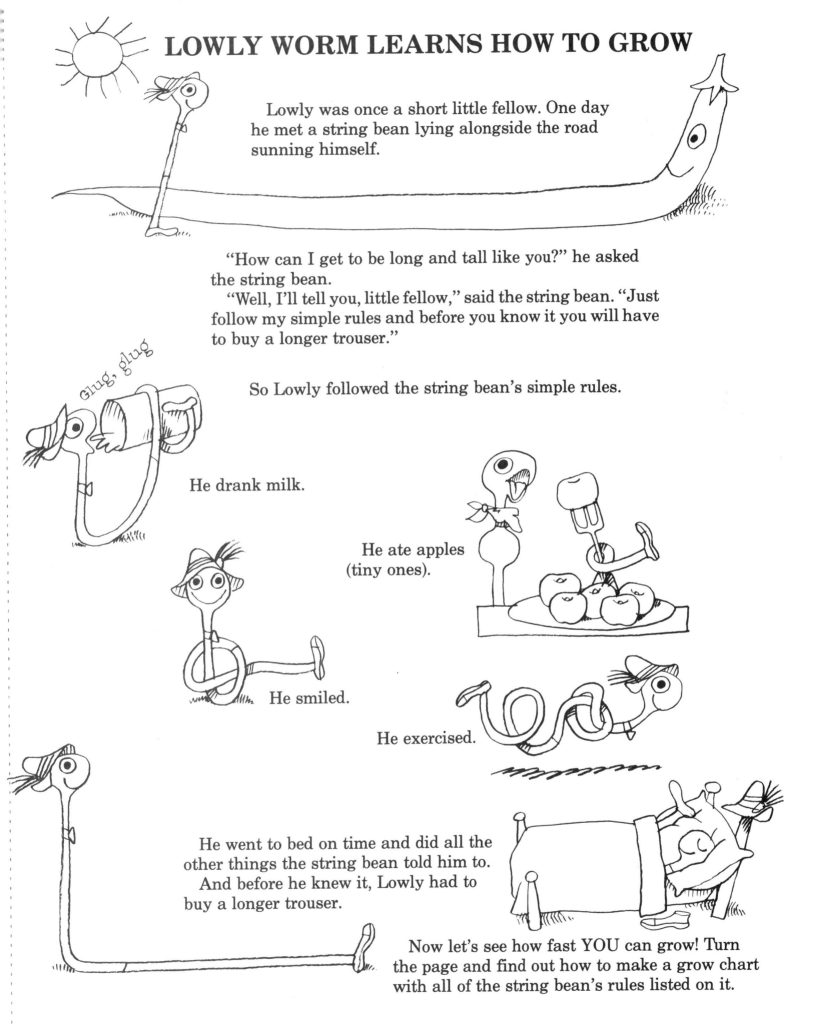

Lowly was once a short little fellow. One day he met a string bean lying alongside the road sunning himself.

"How can I get to be long and tall like you?" he asked the string bean.

"Well, I'll tell you, little fellow," said the string bean. "Just follow my simple rules and before you know it you will have to buy a longer trouser."

So Lowly followed the string bean's simple rules.

Glug, glug

He drank milk.

He ate apples (tiny ones).

He smiled.

He exercised.

He went to bed on time and did all the other things the string bean told him to. And before he knew it, Lowly had to buy a longer trouser.

Now let's see how fast YOU can grow! Turn the page and find out how to make a grow chart with all of the string bean's rules listed on it.

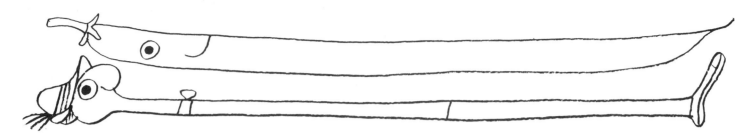

How to make
MY STRING BEAN GROW CHART

1. Color in the next three pages. You might like to use green for the string-bean vine. Then tear out the pages.

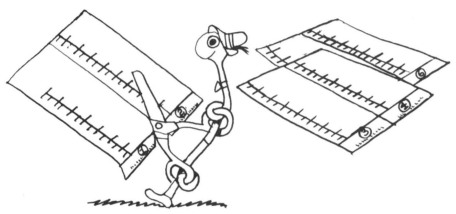

2. Cut the pages in half along the solid black line. You will then have six numbered strips.

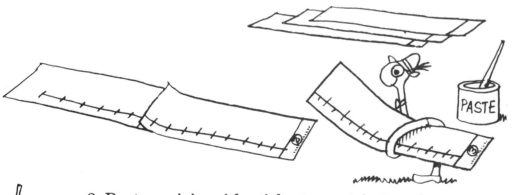

3. Paste, or join with sticky tape: strip 2 to the bottom of strip 1, strip 3 to the bottom of strip 2. Continue until all six strips are joined together.

4. Cut off the bottom piece of strip 6. ⟶

5. Tape or pin your grow chart to a door or wall so that the bottom of the chart just touches the floor.

   Now you can measure yourself growing just like a string-bean vine!

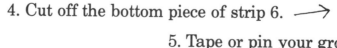

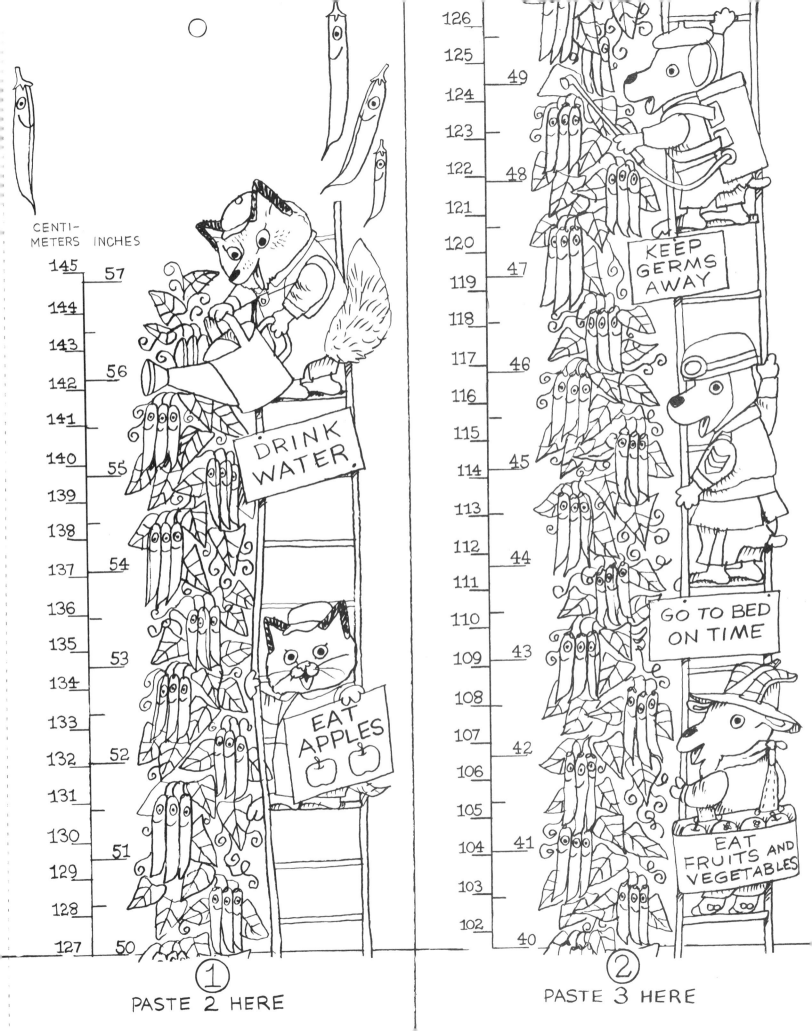

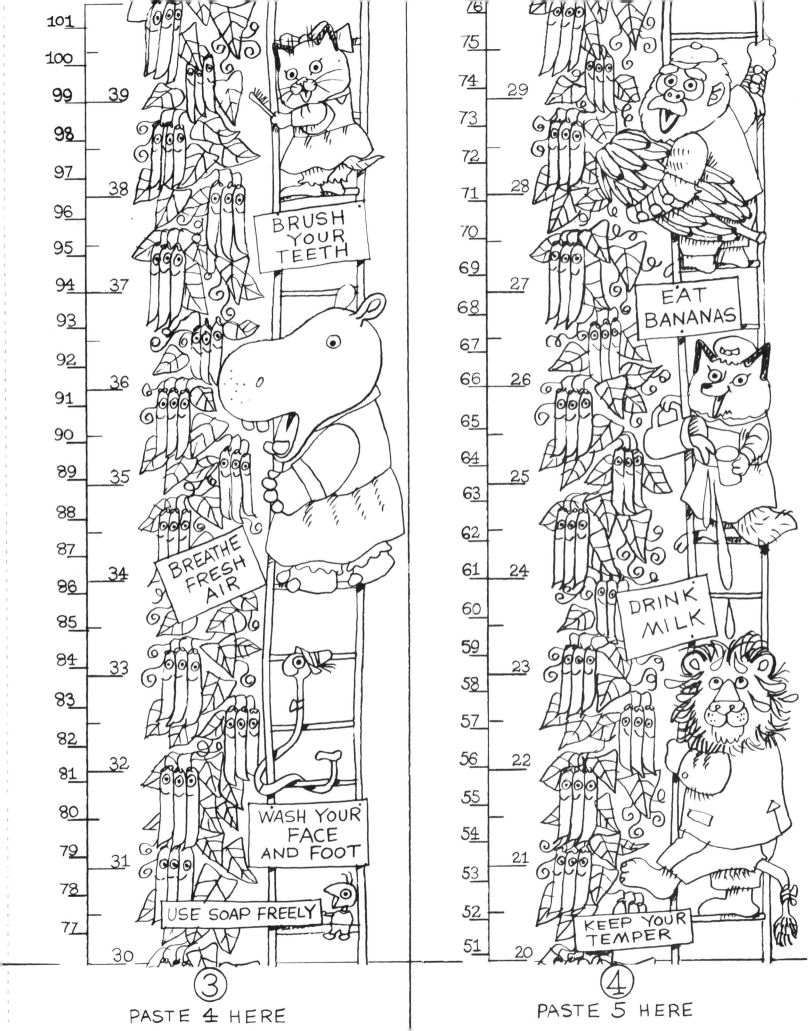

BRUSH YOUR TEETH

BREATHE FRESH AIR

WASH YOUR FACE AND FOOT

USE SOAP FREELY

③

PASTE 4 HERE

EAT BANANAS

DRINK MILK

KEEP YOUR TEMPER

④

PASTE 5 HERE

④ ③

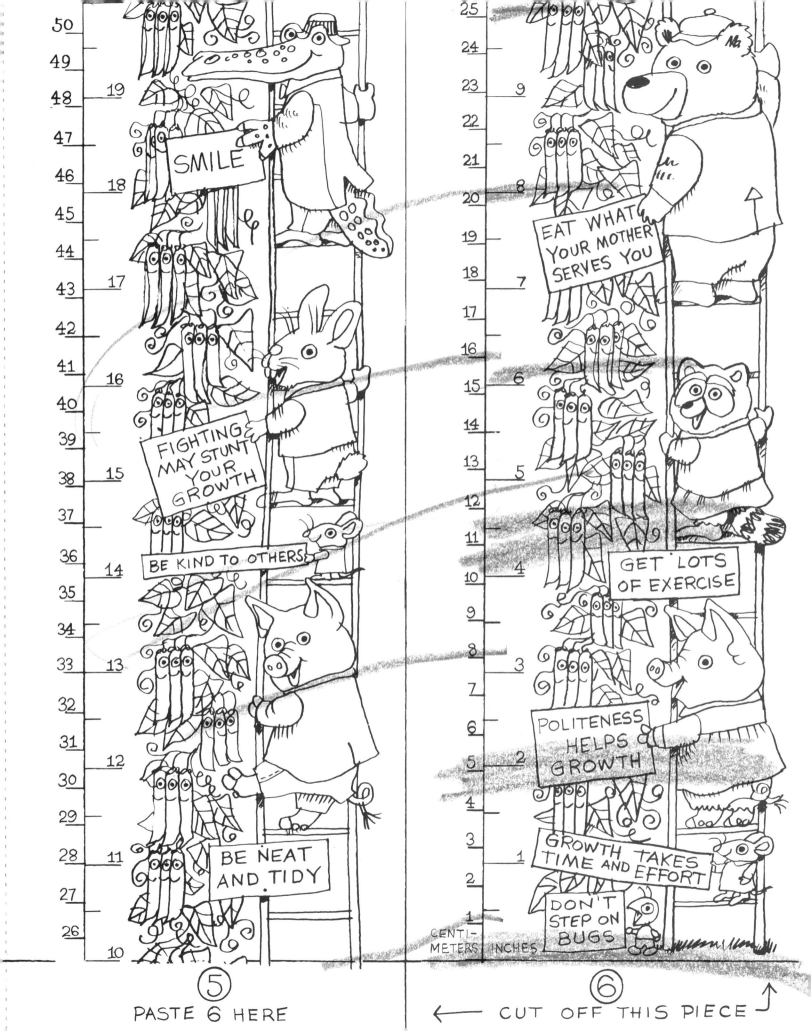

SMILE

FIGHTING MAY STUNT YOUR GROWTH

BE KIND TO OTHERS

BE NEAT AND TIDY

EAT WHAT YOUR MOTHER SERVES YOU

GET LOTS OF EXERCISE

POLITENESS HELPS GROWTH

GROWTH TAKES TIME AND EFFORT

DON'T STEP ON BUGS

CENTI-METERS   INCHES

CHRISTMAS IN BUSYTOWN

Christmas is coming! Everyone is busy getting ready.

Farmer Goat has gone into the woods and chopped down a fine Christmas tree to set up in Busytown Square.

Lots of people are making ornaments to decorate the Christmas tree.

PASTE

Little Sister and Big Tilly are making a chain for the tree.

As everyone sings carols, Lowly
puts the angel on the top of the tree.
Be careful you don't fall, Lowly!

Would you like to have all these Busytown ornaments for your own
tree? You can cut them out on the next few pages.

Color in the ornaments. Remember to use bright, happy colors for
the holidays! Cut along the solid black outlines. Fold along all dotted
lines. With a pencil, gently punch a hole wherever you see ⊗. Tie a
string through each hole so you can hang the ornaments on your tree.

The little pictures on the pages will show you how to put the more
complicated ornaments together.

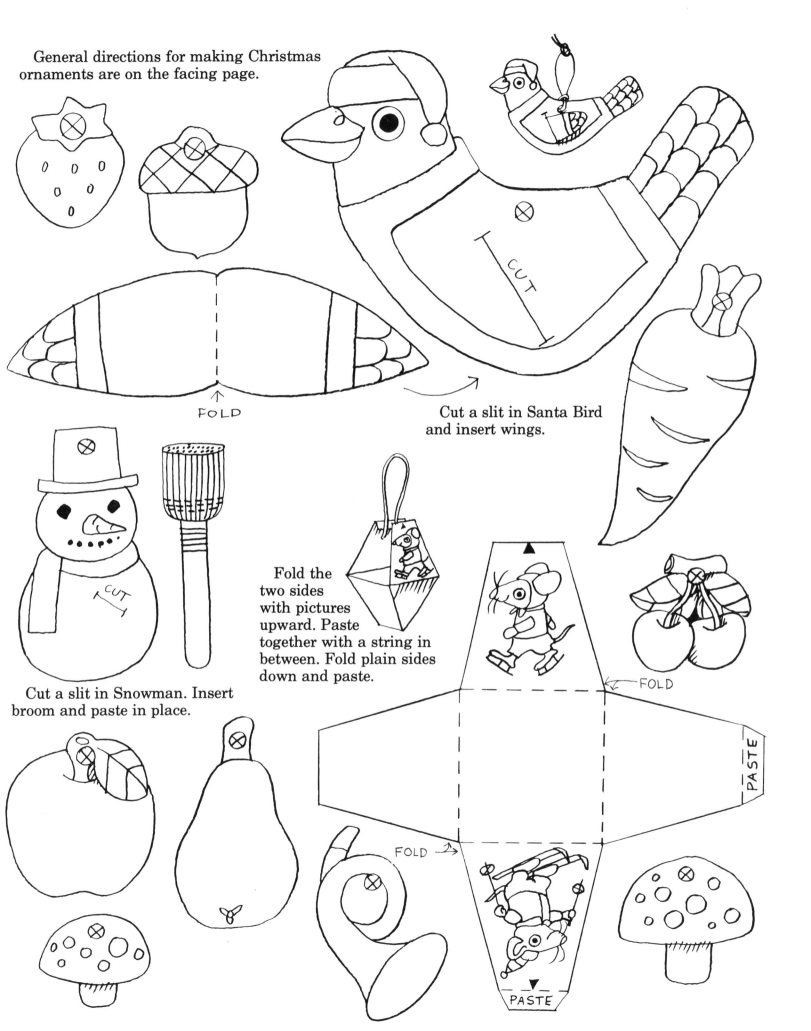

General directions for making Christmas ornaments are on the facing page.

FOLD

Cut a slit in Santa Bird and insert wings.

Fold the two sides with pictures upward. Paste together with a string in between. Fold plain sides down and paste.

Cut a slit in Snowman. Insert broom and paste in place.

CUT

FOLD

PASTE

FOLD

PASTE

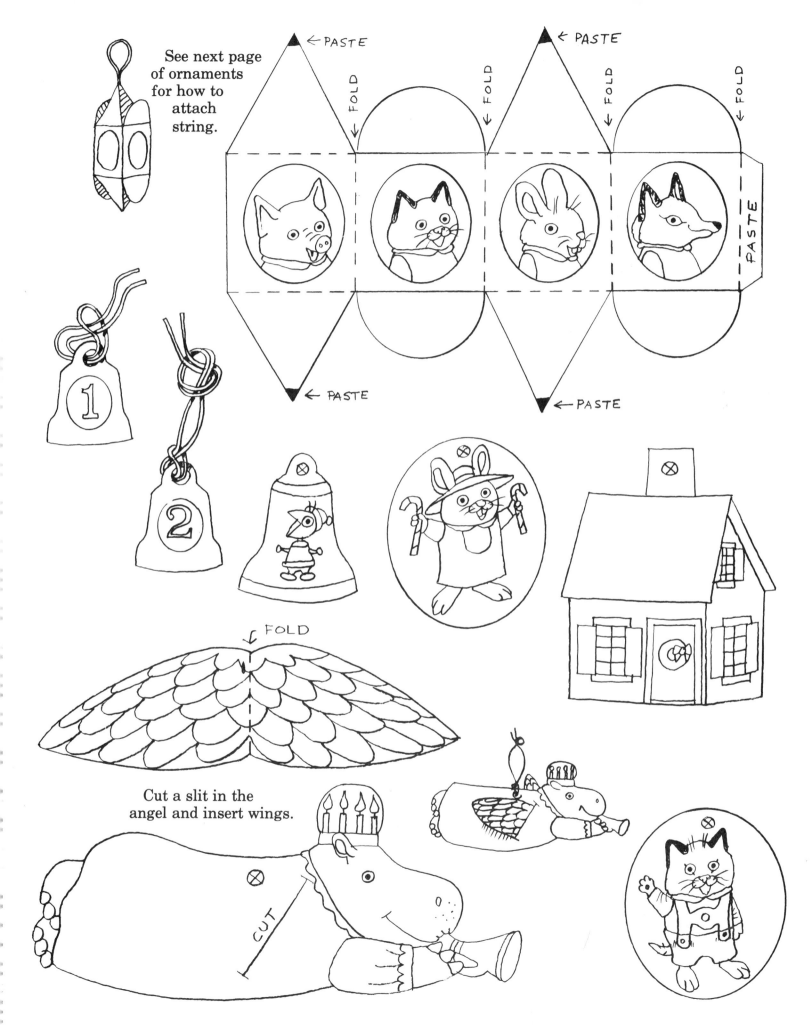

See next page of ornaments for how to attach string.

← PASTE

← PASTE

FOLD

FOLD

FOLD

FOLD

PASTE

← PASTE

← PASTE

1

2

FOLD

Cut a slit in the angel and insert wings.

CUT

Paste side tab first.
Then paste black tips
together, with a string
in between at top.

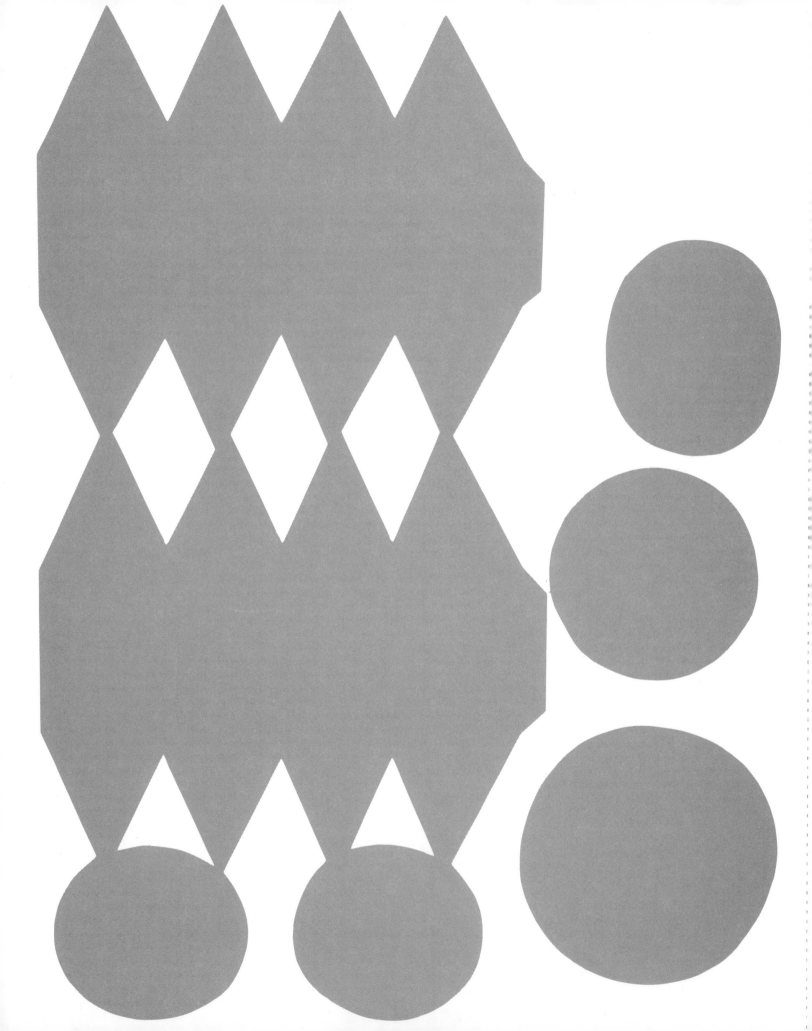

BUG CHAIN

Here is a chain to make for your Christmas tree. Use magic markers, if you have some, to color in the bugs on this and the next page. Tear the pages out. Cut the next page in half to separate the two sets of strips. Then cut all the little strips of bugs apart.

Bend one strip into a loop and paste the ends together. Put a second strip through the first loop and paste its ends together. And so on until all the strips are used up.

Then wind the chain around your Christmas tree.

Merry Christmas!

Don't paste yourself into the chain, Lowly!

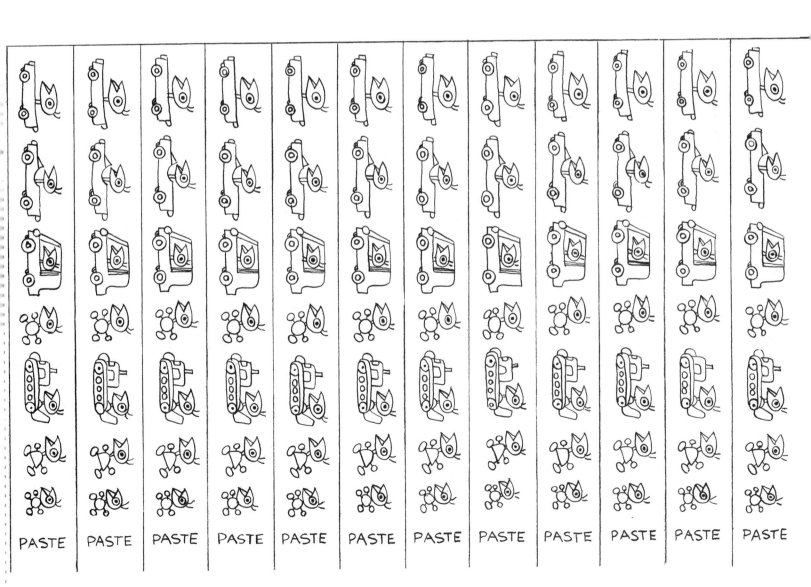

| PASTE | PASTE | PASTE | PASTE | PASTE | PASTE | PASTE | PASTE | PASTE | PASTE | PASTE | PASTE |

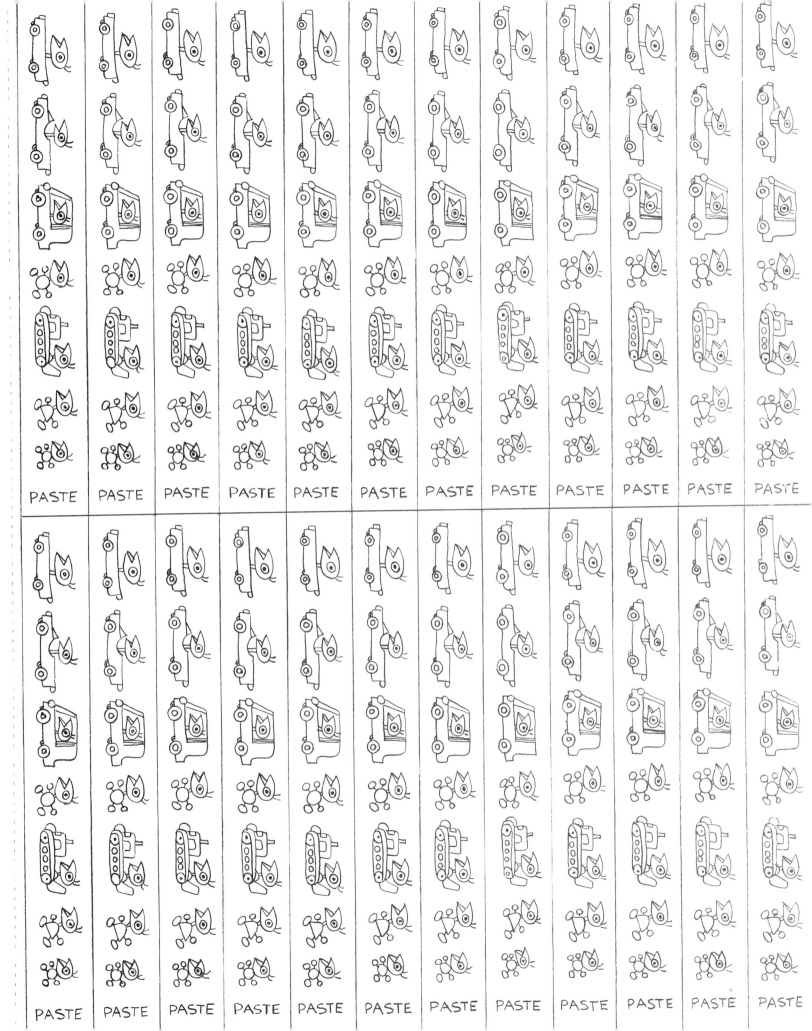

PASTE PASTE PASTE PASTE PASTE PASTE PASTE PASTE PASTE PASTE PASTE PASTE

PASTE PASTE PASTE PASTE PASTE PASTE PASTE PASTE PASTE PASTE PASTE PASTE

THE GINGERBREAD PIG

This is a story about a mischievous gingerbread pig who decides to run away from home! Find out what happens to him and color in the pictures as you go along.

Mommy Pig makes a gingerbread pig for Harry and Sally. She puts him in the oven to bake.

"He must be cooked by now," says Mommy. She opens the oven door and out jumps the gingerbread pig.

He runs out the front door saying, "You can't catch me, I'm the gingerbread pig!"

He runs past Daddy Pig working in the garden.

Come back here!

"You can't catch me, I'm the gingerbread pig!" he calls out. Daddy Pig chases after him, but he can't catch the gingerbread pig.

He comes to Farmer Rabbit riding
on his tractor.
He calls out as he goes by,
"You can't catch me,
I'm the gingerbread pig!"

Farmer Rabbit chases after him,
but he can't catch the gingerbread pig.

Mama Bear is busy knitting.
The gingerbread pig smiles and says,
"You can't catch me,
I'm the gingerbread pig!"
Mama Bear chases after him, but
she can't catch the gingerbread pig.

Then the gingerbread pig comes to
a fox lying by the side of a river.
He says, "You can't catch me,
I'm the gingerbread pig."

But the sly fox just laughs and says,
"If you don't get across this river
quickly, you will surely be caught.
Hop on my tail and I will carry you across."
    The gingerbread pig sees all the people
chasing after him. So he quickly hops
on the fox's tail.

The fox begins to swim across the river.
The gingerbread pig starts to get wet.
So he climbs onto the fox's nose to keep dry.

Then, *snip, snap,* the fox opens his mouth
and eats the gingerbread pig . . .
for that is what gingerbread pigs are for!
And that was the end of the gingerbread pig.

Now you can make your own gingerbread pigs
to eat. Directions are on the next few pages.

YUM!
YUM!

LOWLY'S FAVORITE GINGERBREAD COOKIES

This recipe is Lowly's favorite for making gingerbread pigs. It yields about 6 giant cookies. You can also make the pigs with a packaged gingerbread-cookie mix or your own recipe. You'll need the help of someone who knows how to bake. Remember to always wash your hands before cooking. And be very careful around the hot stove!

You will need:
½ cup (1 stick) butter or margarine, at room temperature
½ cup brown sugar (not Brownulated)
½ cup molasses
2½ cups all-purpose flour

½ teaspoon ground ginger
¼ teaspoon ground cinnamon
⅛ teaspoon ground nutmeg
⅛ teaspoon ground cloves
¼ teaspoon salt
½ teaspoon baking soda

1. Cut out the paper cookie patterns that follow this recipe.

2. Let's start making the dough: Put the butter 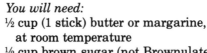 and the brown sugar into a big bowl  and mix them until light and creamy. Then add the molasses and mix until well blended.

3. Get out another bowl 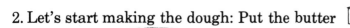 and sift into it the flour 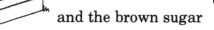, ginger , cinnamon , nutmeg , and cloves, salt , and baking soda . Doesn't the flour smell delicious with all those fragrant spices in it?

4. Add the sifted flour and spices to the mixture in the big bowl and stir well. You will end up with a crumbly mixture. Lowly says it's easier to add the flour ½ cup at a time, mixing it in well before adding more. (Do you know how many half-cups there are in 2½ cups? The answer is 5!)

5. Now turn on the oven and set it at 375° . It will heat to the right temperature while you finish the dough and roll out the cookies.

6. With your hands (make sure they're clean!), knead and press the crumbly mixture in the bowl until it becomes a ball of dough. Isn't it fun to feel all the little crumbles stick together?

7. Now the dough is ready to be rolled out. Lowly says to sprinkle the rolling pin with flour before you start. That will keep the dough from sticking to the pin.

8. Roll out about a third of the dough directly onto an ungreased baking sheet. The dough should be about ⅛ inch thick. Place a paper pattern on dough, color side up. It will stick in place. (You may be able to fit on the second pattern, too.) Carefully cut through the dough with a knife, going all around the pattern.

9. Carefully lift up and remove the extra dough around the cookie. It can be rerolled later.

10. Now mark areas on the cookie that will later be filled in with frosting. With a toothpick or poultry skewer, gently prick holes along the black lines on pattern, going through pattern and cookie dough.

11. Carefully peel off the paper pattern.

12. Bake cookie for 10 to 12 minutes, or until lightly browned. Cut more cookies while the first one bakes. Cool off the first baking sheet before rolling more dough on it.

13. If you plan to hang the cookies on a Christmas tree, carefully make holes in them with a toothpick as soon as they come out of the oven. They'll be soft then.

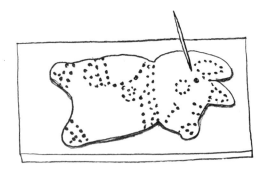

14. Let the cookies cool completely before frosting them. Directions for "painting" the pigs with frosting are on the page following the paper cookie patterns.

15. AND REMEMBER! Never let your gingerbread pig run away from you!

Patterns for gingerbread cookies.

FROSTING "PAINT" FOR GINGERBREAD COOKIES

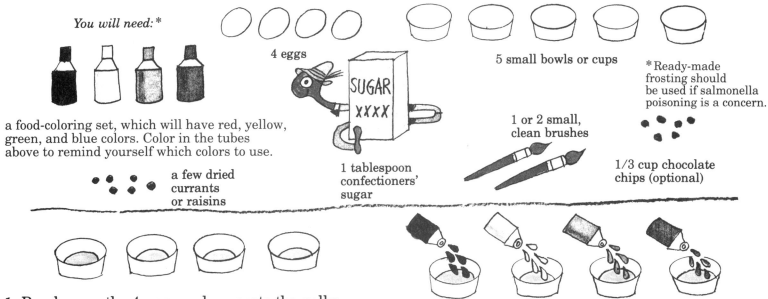

You will need: *

a food-coloring set, which will have red, yellow, green, and blue colors. Color in the tubes above to remind yourself which colors to use.

a few dried currants or raisins

4 eggs

1 tablespoon confectioners' sugar

5 small bowls or cups

1 or 2 small, clean brushes

* Ready-made frosting should be used if salmonella poisoning is a concern.

1/3 cup chocolate chips (optional)

1. Break open the 4 eggs and separate the yolks from the whites. Put each yolk in a separate bowl. Save the whites for another use.

2. Add about 5 drops of food coloring to each yolk, one color to a yolk. Mix well. (What happens when you add blue food coloring to a yellow yolk? It turns dark green! The yolk with green food coloring will turn light green.)

3. Put the tablespoon of confectioners' sugar in the fifth bowl. Add a few drops of water, and stir to make a thick paste.

4. As soon as your cookies are cool, "paint" them with the colored yolks, using a brush. You will have 4 colors of paint—red, yellow, light green, and dark green. Try painting Gingerbread Pig's shirt yellow and his overalls red, or make up your own color combinations. When you finish with each color, rinse out your paintbrush and shake off the excess water.

5. To make eyes, dab a drop of sugar paste on the cookie where the eye should be. Then press a dried currant or bit of raisin into the paste.

6. If you wish to make outlines on the cookies after the "paint" is dry, melt 1/3 cup of chocolate chips in a double boiler.

7. Then, with a toothpick or brush, draw outlines, noses, whiskers, etc., with the melted chocolate. Put the cookies in the refrigerator to harden the chocolate.

8. Lowly says the paint colors will be especially bright if you put on two layers. Just remember to let the first layer of paint dry thoroughly before you put on the second.

LOWLY WORM'S BIRTHDAY PARTY

Lowly is going to have a birthday party. He makes invitation cards and mails them to all his friends.

On the day of the party all his friends come bringing birthday presents.

But where is Sergeant Murphy? He was invited but he hasn't come. Well, we can't wait for him.

My, what a beautiful cake! But before we eat it, Lowly must blow out all the candles.
Take a deep breath, Lowly . . . and BLOW!

OH, LOWLY!
You blew too hard!
Lowly's birthday cake blew out the window.

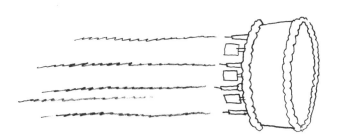

Ah! Here comes Sergeant Murphy now.
What will he bring to the party, I wonder?

Sergeant Murphy brings a
birthday cake to the party.

YUM
YUM!

It is not very beautiful anymore,
but it is *still* a birthday cake.
And it still tastes good, too.
How does your piece taste,
Sergeant Murphy?

LOWLY'S BEST BIRTHDAY CAKE
CREAMY ORANGE FROSTING EVER

Here is the recipe for Lowly's own birthday cake frosting, for you to make with your mom or dad. It will cover and fill a 9-inch, 2-layer cake. You can put this frosting on any kind of cake you like. Then decorate your cake with the birthday cake cutouts on the next page.

You will need: *
½ cup (1 stick) butter or margarine, at room temperature
1 box (16 oz.) confectioners' sugar
1 egg
3 tablespoons orange juice
¼ teaspoon orange flavoring (optional)
1 tablespoon grated orange rind (optional)

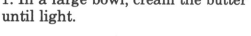

1. In a large bowl, cream the butter until light.

2. Into a second bowl, sift all the confectioners' sugar.

3. SLOWLY add ½ cup of the sifted sugar to the butter, stirring as you add it. Mix until smooth.

4. Add the egg to the butter-sugar mixture and blend well.

5. Now add the rest of the sifted sugar, about one cup at a time, alternating with 1 tablespoon of orange juice at a time. Blend well after each addition.

* Ready-made frosting should be used if salmonella poisoning is a concern.

6. If you wish, add orange flavoring and grated orange rind to the frosting. Lowly always does—the flavor is DELICIOUS!

7. Frost your cake when it is completely cool after baking.

8. Don't forget to lick the frosting bowl. Lowly never forgets!

9. Lowly also likes to add squiggles of stiff, decorative white frosting to his cake. If you want to add them, you'll need: 1 stick butter or margarine; 2 cups confectioners' sugar, sifted after measuring; 3 teaspoons milk; ¼ teaspoon orange flavoring. Cream the butter. Slowly add half the sugar, mixing it in well. Add remaining sugar and the milk in alternate thirds, blending well.

Add orange flavoring. Spoon frosting into a decorating tube. Pipe frosting onto cake so that it looks like the one on page 90. Any extra frosting may be frozen for later use.

10. Now your cake is ready to be decorated with all the little birthday figures on page 91. Turn this page for directions.

BIRTHDAY PARTY INVITATIONS

After the next page, you will see two pages of birthday party invitations. Color the animals you see on the invitations. Then tear out the pages. Cut the invitations apart. Address them. Write down the day, time, and place of the party. Then sign your name.

Fold the invitations and seal them at one end with tape, as the picture shows. Stick a stamp on each one.

Drop your birthday party invitations in the mail! Have a nice party!

BIRTHDAY CAKE DECORATIONS

Color in the decorations on the facing page. Cut them out, following the solid black outlines.

Also cut some straws into pieces about 3 or 4 inches long. You'll need 12 pieces in all.

The smaller decorations are age markers. In the circles on the markers, write how old you'll be on your birthday.

On the center decoration, write your name under "Happy Birthday," front and back.

To put the decorations together, follow the pictures and instructions on this page. Then decorate your cake. Make sure that you leave some room between the markers and the candles.

The decorations are NOT to be used as candleholders. Buy candles and candleholders at the store to make your birthday cake the Prettiest Birthday Cake Ever.

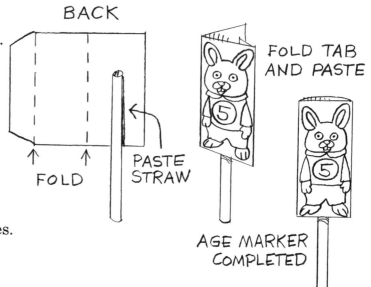

AGE MARKERS
BACK

FOLD TAB AND PASTE

FOLD

PASTE STRAW

AGE MARKER COMPLETED

CENTER DECORATION

FRONT

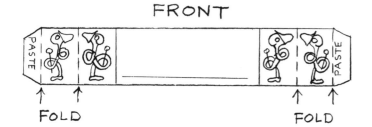

PASTE

FOLD

FOLD

PASTE

BACK

PASTE STRAWS HERE

BACK

TABS ARE FOLDED UNDER AND PASTED DOWN

FRONT

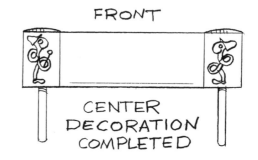

CENTER DECORATION COMPLETED

This is the age Lowly put on his age marker. What a clown he is! Come now, Lowly! You're not 101 years old!

This is what Lowly's cake looks like when it is all decorated.

PASTE

PASTE

PASTE

PASTE

PASTE

PASTE

PASTE

PASTE

PASTE

PASTE

PASTE

PASTE

Happy Birthday

FOLD ON THE
DOTTED LINES

Happy Birthday

Mollie

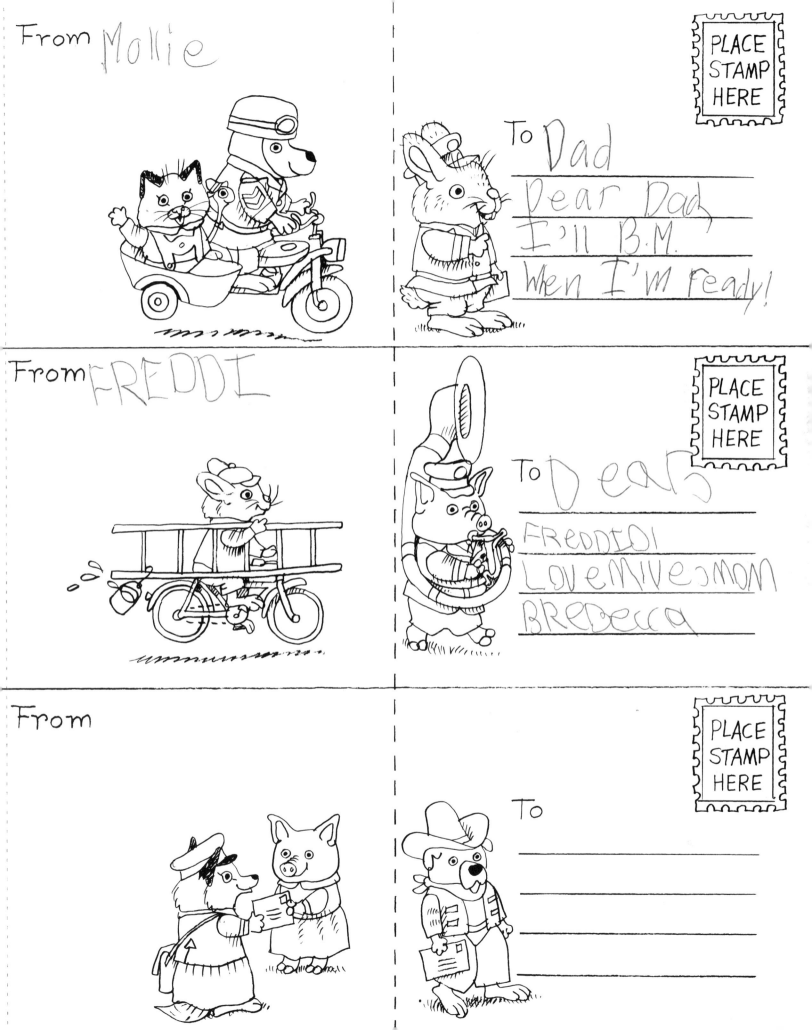

From Mollie

To Dad
Dear Dad,
I'll B.M.
When I'm ready!

From FREDDI

To DeaR
FReDDIDI
LoveMiveJMoM
BReDecca

From

To

Please come to my birthday party

ON _____
DATE

AT _____
TIME

at my house

_____

_____
ADDRESS

DAD
MOllie   NAME

Please come to my birthday party

ON _____
DATE

AT _____
TIME

at my house

_____

_____
ADDRESS

Rebecca   NAME

Please come to my birthday party

ON _____
DATE

AT _____
TIME

at my house

_____

_____
ADDRESS

Mom   NAME

From

PLACE STAMP HERE

To MOM
Dear MOM,
I love you
love,
Mollie

From

PLACE STAMP HERE

To

From

PLACE STAMP HERE

To

Please come to my birthday party

ON _____
DATE

AT _____
TIME

at my house

_____

_____
ADDRESS

_____
NAME

Please come to my birthday party

ON _____
DATE

AT _____
TIME

at my house

_____

_____
ADDRESS

_____
NAME

Please come to my birthday party

ON _____
DATE

AT_____
TIME

at my house

_____

_____
ADDRESS

_____
NAME

THE ADVENTURES OF LOWLY WORM

I am Lowly Worm. I have many friends. I help my friend Sergeant Murphy direct traffic.

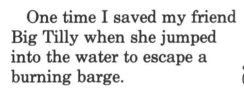

One time I saved my friend Big Tilly when she jumped into the water to escape a burning barge.

My best friend is Huckle Cat. We once sang on television together.

Bananas Gorilla is my friend—when he is good.

Sometimes he is bad and steals bananas. I once captured Bananas when he was stealing bananas. Sergeant Murphy put him in jail to teach him a lesson.

I try to be good but sometimes I am a little naughty.

Hold still, Lowly!

I once fell in a mud puddle and tracked mud all over Mrs. Cat's floor.

She had to give me a bath. I am very slippery in the bathtub.

I peel apples for Huckle's grandmother when she comes to visit Huckle.

Grandma makes SUPER apple pies.

I like to play "Pin the Tail on the Donkey" at birthday parties.

Once someone pinned a donkey tail on me. Wasn't I a silly-looking donkey?

I always try to be polite. I thank my friends and their mothers when I am leaving their house after a visit. I say, "Thank you for the very nice time."

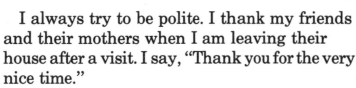

When my friends get sick, I send them a card telling them I hope they get well soon.

I once took a space trip to the moon. I brought the spaceship safely back to earth. I got a medal for being a good astro-knot.

I am a very busy fellow. Once I helped Smokey, the fireman, rescue Huckle from a burning house. That was exciting!

I go to bed when I am told. (But sometimes I have to be told twice!) I like to take my very own Lowly Worm doll to bed with me.

Wouldn't you like to take a Lowly Worm doll to bed, too? On the next two pages you will find out how to make your own Lowly Worm doll.

Good night!

LOWLY WORM DOLL

To make Lowly, you'll need the help of someone who knows how to sew. You can sew Lowly by hand or on a sewing machine. Be careful with your sewing scissors, pins, and needles! If you have a sewing machine, be very careful around it, too.

Materials needed: For the main parts of Lowly: tan, blue, and green felt. Precut pieces of felt are sold in many fabric stores and sewing departments. If they measure at least 8 inches by 10 inches, you can use them for Lowly. Or buy ¼ yard each of tan, blue, and green felt.

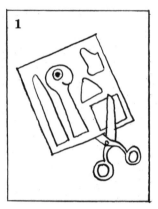

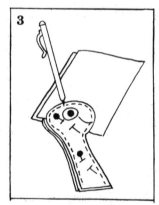
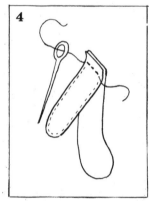

1. First color the pattern pieces, following the coloring directions printed on each pattern piece. Then cut out all the pattern pieces along the solid black outlines.

2. Pin each pattern piece to felt of the matching color. If the pattern says "cut 2," fold felt in half and pin pattern to two layers at once. Cut out the felt along the edge of pattern. The eyes and pupils will be easier to cut if you just trace around the patterns with a pencil, then cut out the felt along your pencil line.

3. Transfer seam lines on pattern pieces to felt: Slip carbon paper face down between pattern and felt. If there are two layers of felt, put another piece of carbon paper face up beneath the bottom layer. Trace along seam lines (dotted lines) on pattern with a ball-point pen. Press firmly. Then unpin the pattern pieces.

4. With right sides together (with the clean, unmarked sides facing each other), stitch one head to one trouser along the seam line. Trim seam close to stitching. (Picture 5 shows how to trim a seam.) Repeat with other head and trouser.

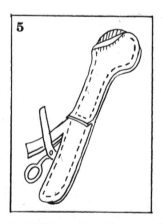
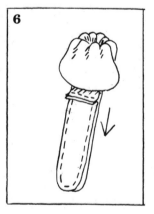
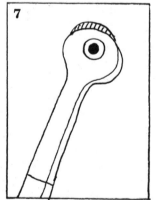
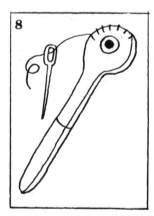

5. With right sides together, stitch the halves of Lowly together along the seam lines. Leave head open as marked on pattern. Trim seam close to stitching.

6. Turn Lowly right side out.

7. Glue pupils to eyes and eyes to head, using pattern as placement guide.

8. Stuff doll firmly. Poke the stuffing down into Lowly's trouser with the handle of a wooden kitchen spoon. Trim ⅛ inch off open edges of head. Sew head-opening shut.

To trim Lowly: scraps of white, black, red, brown, and yellow felt; 4 tiny pearl buttons; a small feather. Thread: any color for inner seams; red, brown, and green for exposed stitching. Use Dacron stuffing inside Lowly; a one-pound bag is more than enough.

Other materials: a pencil, typewriter carbon paper (or dressmaker's tracing paper), a ball-point pen (or dressmaker's tracing wheel), white glue (or fabric glue), a black felt-tip marking pen.

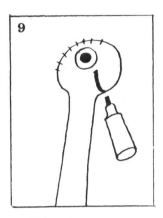 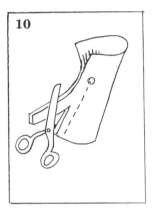 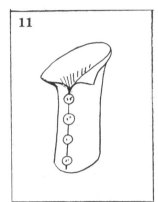 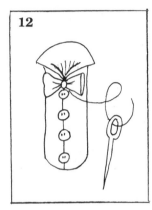

9. Using the pattern as a guide, carefully draw mouth with black marking pen.

10. Lightly fold the jacket in half to bring the sides together. Stitch the sides together as far as the dot on the pattern. Trim seam past the dot all the way to top of jacket.

11. Turn jacket right side out. Sew buttons on along seam line. Leave room at top of seam for bow tie.

12. To make bow tie, cut a piece of red felt 1 inch by ½ inch. Tie felt in middle with red thread. Sew bow tie to jacket.

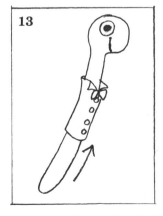 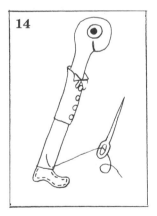 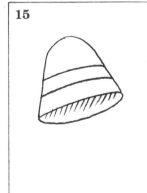 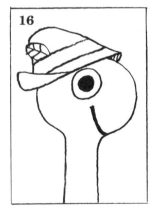

13. Put jacket on Lowly from the bottom.

14. Stitch the two pieces of the shoe together, using brown thread. Leave open at top. Trim seam. Do *not* turn shoe inside out. Slip shoe on Lowly's leg and secure with a few tiny stitches.

15. With right sides together, stitch the two pieces of hat together with green thread. Trim seam. Turn hat right side out. For the hatband, cut a strip of yellow felt ⅛ inch wide and 5½ inches long. Overlap the ends ¼ inch and glue together. When dry, put band on hat.

16. Glue a small feather between hat and hatband. Secure band to hat with a few tiny stitches. Put hat on Lowly and turn up back brim.

Now you have your very own Lowly Worm to play with!

COLOR LOWLY WORM

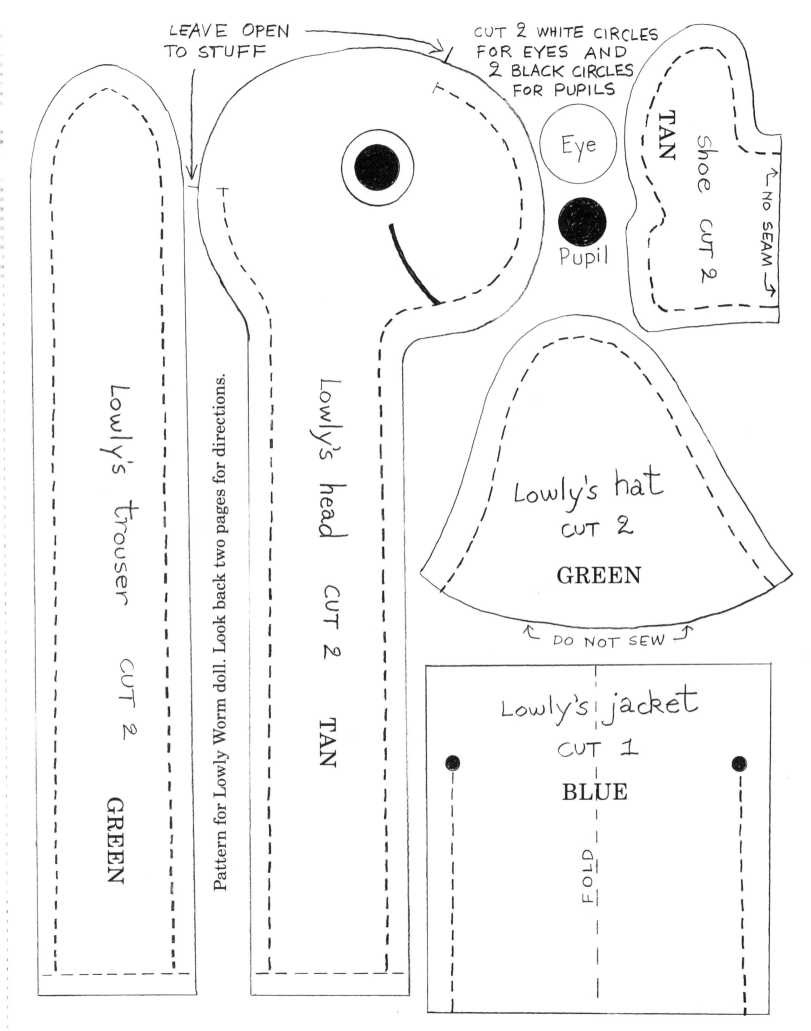

LEAVE OPEN
TO STUFF

CUT 2 WHITE CIRCLES
FOR EYES AND
2 BLACK CIRCLES
FOR PUPILS

Eye

Pupil

TAN

Shoe CUT 2

NO SEAM

Lowly's trouser CUT 2

GREEN

Pattern for Lowly Worm doll. Look back two pages for directions.

Lowly's head CUT 2 TAN

Lowly's hat
CUT 2
GREEN

DO NOT SEW

Lowly's jacket
CUT 1
BLUE

FOLD

MS. MOUSE

Ms. Mouse is a very busy mouse.
Help color in her busy day.

She paints houses.

She fixes
leaking water pipes.

She fixes cars that won't run.

She drives the school bus.

She is a very brave volunteer firefighter
who puts out fires.

She likes to do all these things but . . .

. . . but best of all, Ms. Mouse likes to make dolls for her friends.

Now, how would you like to make a
Ms. Mouse doll for yourself?
The next two pages will tell you how.

LET'S MAKE MS. MOUSE!

You'll need the help of someone who can sew to make this felt doll. You can sew Ms. Mouse by hand or on a sewing machine. Be careful with sewing scissors, pins, and needles! If you have a sewing machine at your house, be very careful around it, too.

Materials needed: For the main parts of Ms. Mouse, yellow and light brown felt. Precut felt pieces are sold in many fabric stores and sewing departments. If they measure at least 5 by 10 inches, you can use them for Ms. Mouse. Or buy ¼ yard

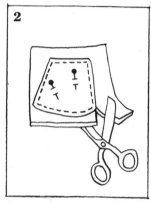

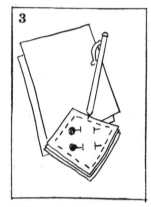

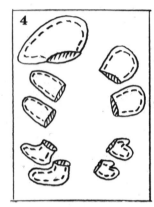

1. First color the pattern pieces, following the coloring directions printed on each pattern piece. Then cut out all the pattern pieces along the solid black outlines.

2. Put pattern pieces for eyes, nose, tail, and handle on felt of the matching color. Trace around each pattern with a pencil. If the pattern says "cut 2," trace around it twice. Cut out the felt along your pencil lines.
   Pin all other pattern pieces to doubled-over felt of the matching color. Cut out the felt along the edge of pattern. If the pattern says "cut 4," pin and cut again.

3. Transfer the seam lines (the dotted lines) on pattern pieces to felt: Slip carbon paper face down between pattern and felt. Put another piece of carbon paper face up beneath bottom layer of felt. Trace along seam lines on pattern with a ball-point pen. Press firmly. Also trace the face markings on head. Then unpin the pattern pieces.

4. Using light brown thread, stitch the two pieces for head together along the seam line. Leave head open at one end as picture 4 shows. Trim seam close to stitching (trim off extra felt next to stitching, as shown on page 100, picture 5). Do *not* turn felt inside out. Repeat this step to make the ears, sleeves, hands, and feet, using thread of a matching color.

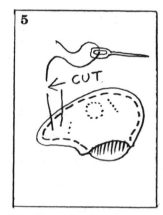

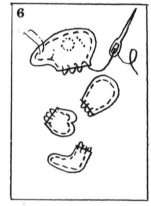

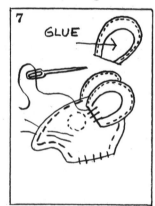

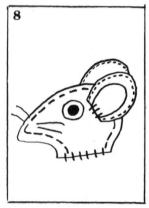

5. To make whiskers: Thread a needle with black thread and knot it at one end. Bring needle up from inside the head near nose (see pattern). Clip thread to about ½ inch long. Make two whiskers on each side of head.

6. Lightly stuff head, ears, hands, and feet. Don't try to make them round; they should just bulge slightly. Sew all openings shut.

7. Glue or sew a pink inner ear to each ear. Sew ears to head.

8. Glue black pupils to white eyes, and glue eyes to head.

each of yellow and light brown felt. You'll also need: scraps of pink, white, black, and dark brown felt; a bunch of tiny artificial flowers; yellow, light brown, black, and white thread. Use Dacron stuffing inside Ms. Mouse; you'll need only a small part of a one-pound bag.

Other things to have on hand: a pencil, typewriter carbon paper (or dressmaker's tracing paper), a ball-point pen (or dressmaker's tracing wheel), white glue (or fabric glue), a black felt-tip marking pen.

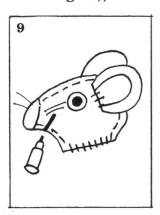

9. Glue nose to head, one piece on each side. Draw mouth with a black marking pen.

10. Using yellow thread, stitch the two pieces of dress together along the side seams only. Leave an opening to insert the tail later. Trim seam close to stitching. Insert head about ⅜ inch into neck opening. Pin in place. Stitch across top of dress along seam line, joining head to dress. Trim seam.

11. Lightly stuff the dress. Insert feet about ⅜ inch into bottom opening, where marked on pattern. Pin in place. Stitch across bottom of dress, joining feet to dress. Trim seam.

12. Lightly stuff the sleeves. Insert hands into sleeve openings and sew hands to sleeves. Sew finished arms to dress at shoulders.

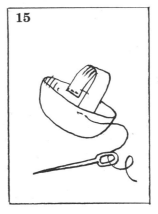

13. Stitch the two pieces of collar together along the seam line. Trim seam. Turn collar inside out, place around neck, and sew to dress with white thread.

14. Insert tail about ¼ inch into side opening of dress. Stitch in place along side seam line, using yellow thread.

15. Stitch basket pieces together. Turn inside out. Sew or glue handle to basket.

16. Sew or glue flowers to inside of basket. Slip basket on Ms. Mouse's arm, and you are done!

If any marking lines for seams show, remove by gently rubbing with an eraser or damp cloth.

COLOR MS. MOUSE

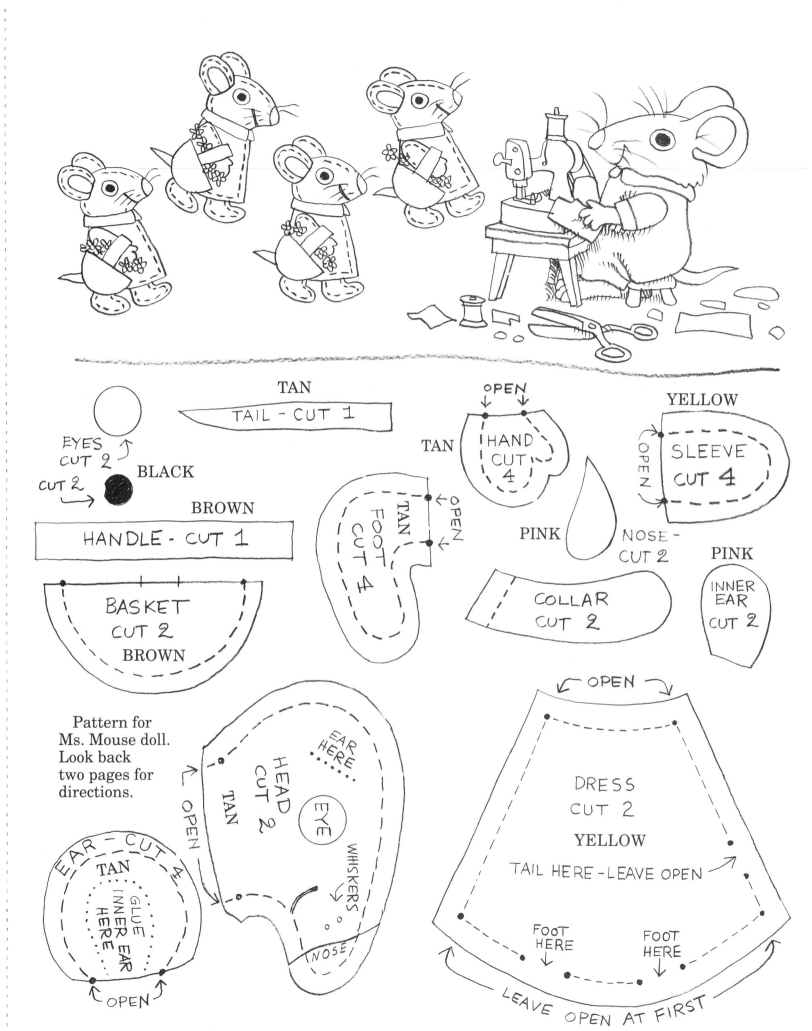

TAN

TAIL - CUT 1

EYES
CUT 2

CUT 2 → BLACK

BROWN

HANDLE - CUT 1

BASKET
CUT 2

BROWN

TAN
FOOT
CUT 4

← OPEN

OPEN ↓ ↓

TAN

HAND
CUT
4

PINK

NOSE -
CUT 2

COLLAR
CUT 2

YELLOW

OPEN

SLEEVE
CUT 4

PINK

INNER
EAR
CUT 2

Pattern for
Ms. Mouse doll.
Look back
two pages for
directions.

EAR - CUT 4

TAN

GLUE
INNER
EAR
HERE

← OPEN →

OPEN

HEAD
CUT 2

TAN

EAR
HERE

EYE

WHISKERS

NOSE

OPEN

DRESS
CUT 2

YELLOW

TAIL HERE - LEAVE OPEN →

FOOT
HERE
↓

FOOT
HERE
↓

LEAVE OPEN AT FIRST

Mr. Paint Pig says, "Sam Cat and Dudley Pig are good friends. They work together as detectives. Please color them. Maybe you can find a mystery for them to solve, too."

HUCKLE HAND PUPPET

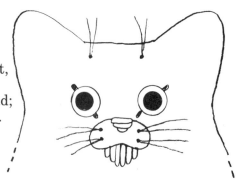

Materials needed: Light brown felt, 9 by 12 inches; yellow and blue felt, 4 by 5 inches each; scraps of black felt; pearl cotton thread #5 or heavy-duty thread in pink, red, and black; light brown and black sewing thread; carbon paper; ballpoint pen (or dressmaker's tracing wheel); white glue.

1. Color the pattern pieces on the facing page, following the coloring directions printed on each pattern piece. Cut out pattern pieces. With a pencil, trace around smaller pieces on felt of matching color. Pin larger pieces to felt of matching color. (Fold brown felt in half first.) Cut out all felt.

2. Slip carbon paper between pattern and top piece of brown felt. Transfer seam line and facial features to felt by tracing along them with a ball-point pen. Unpin all pattern pieces.

3. Glue pupils to eyes, and eyes to face. Glue muzzle to face. Using heavy thread, stitch a black line on either side of each eye, and stitch a pink nose and red tongue with many stitches close together. Make whiskers on muzzle and forehead by bringing a double length of black sewing thread, knotted at the end, through felt from behind; clip to about ½ inch long.

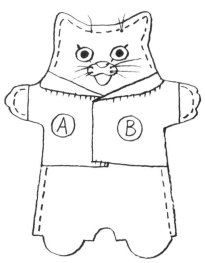

4. Stitch the two pieces of body together along seam line, using light brown thread. Leave bottom open as shown. Face will be on the outside.

5. Fold down collar of shirt A and glue in place. Glue shirt A to body.

6. Glue down collar of shirt B. Glue B to body, overlapping A.

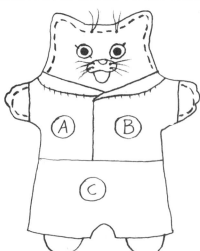

7. Glue pants C to body, overlapping shirt.

8. Cut out (or punch out with a hole-puncher) 8 small circles of black felt. Glue on paws as shown. Cut out 4 circles of yellow felt and 6 circles of blue felt for buttons. Glue to pants and shirt. With heavy black thread, stitch around ears and make 3 long stitches on toes, as shown.

Slip your hand into the puppet and make Huckle Cat talk!

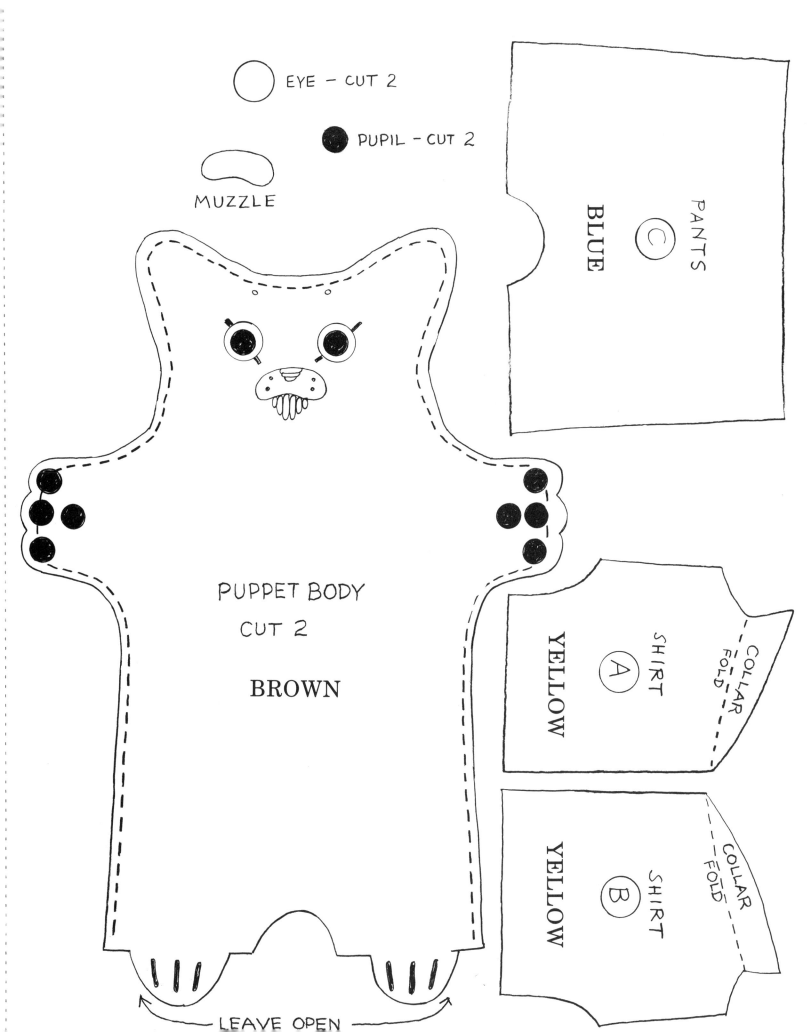

TANGLEFOOT HELPS THE EASTER BUNNY

Knock! Knock!
Someone was knocking on Mrs. Rabbit's door.
It was the Easter Bunny.
"I am looking for someone to help me make chocolate Easter bunnies," he said.

"Why, my little boy Tanglefoot will be happy to help you," said Mrs. Rabbit.
"Tanglefoot," she called. "Go along with the Easter Bunny and help him. And please bring me back one of the chocolate Easter bunnies that you make."

Tanglefoot went off with the Easter Bunny. They melted huge blocks of chocolate. They poured the chocolate into molds and made hundreds and hundreds of chocolate Easter bunnies.

Now and then Tanglefoot spilled some of the melted chocolate. Be careful, Tanglefoot!
Finally all of the chocolate bunnies were made. The Easter Bunny gave one of them to Tanglefoot.

For you, Mama!

When Tanglefoot arrived home, his mother was very surprised.
"Oh, my," she said. "I asked for only one chocolate bunny but I seem to see two of them!"

"I think I will put one bunny on the table—and the other one in the bathtub!" She gave Tanglefoot a big kiss. My, he tasted good!
Happy Easter to the real live chocolate Easter Bunny!

EASTER EGG HOLDERS

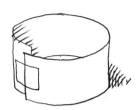

1. Color and then cut out the pieces on the facing page. Join the ends of the long strips together with paste or tape to make the bases for your holders.

2. Paste or tape each animal to the back of a base.

3. Your egg holder will look like this.

4. Ask your mother or father to hard-boil four eggs for you.

   Decorate the eggs with paints or crayons. The pictures below show some designs that you can copy. Or think up your own designs.

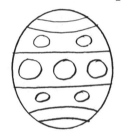

5. Place each decorated egg in a holder. Happy Easter from the Easter Bunny!

PASTE OR TAPE ENDS TOGETHER

| PASTE | PASTE | PASTE | PASTE |

Mr. Paint Pig says, "Here is a picture of Mama Bear for you to color. Please give her a blue book and draw some flowers on her dress."

Mr Paint Pig

STORIES

Please read to me!

THE TV MOVIE

Telly and Vizzy sat in their TV news truck. They were waiting for something to happen so they could film it for a TV show. Sergeant Murphy saw them. He parked his motorcycle and said to them, "Can't you read the 'No Parking' sign? Why, even my motorcycle could read that!"

I think Sergeant Murphy's motorcycle must have heard him. It is starting to run away.

"Chase after it!" shouted Telly. "This will make an exciting film for television!"

To see the film that Telly and Vizzy made, follow the directions that you will find two pages on.

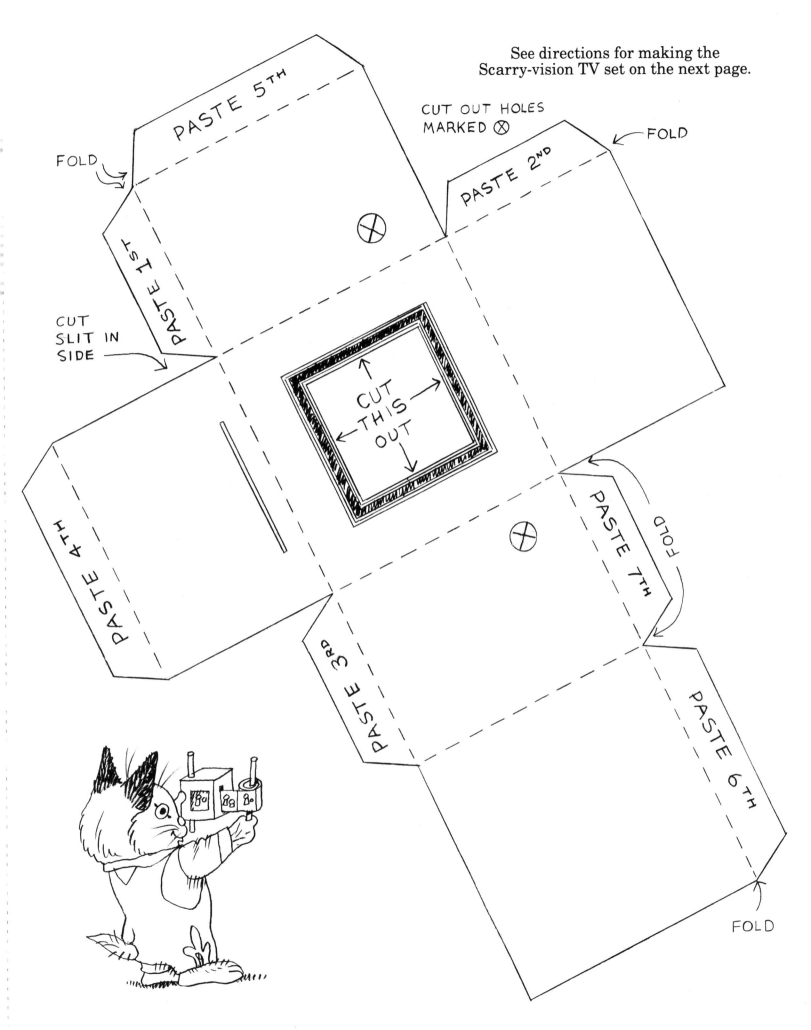

See directions for making the
Scarry-vision TV set on the next page.

CUT OUT HOLES
MARKED ⊗

FOLD

PASTE 5TH

FOLD

PASTE 2ND

PASTE 1ST

CUT
SLIT IN
SIDE

CUT
THIS
OUT

PASTE 4TH

PASTE 7TH

FOLD

PASTE 3RD

PASTE 6TH

FOLD

SCARRY-VISION

1. Color and then cut out the TV set on the page before this one. Cut out screen, slit, and holes. Fold along dotted lines. Don't paste yet.

2. Color and then cut out the three "film" strips on this page. Paste strips together so that strips 1 and 3 overlap strip 2, as shown.

3. Cut two straws about 5 inches long. Paste the end of strip 1 to the middle of one straw. Wind the film up on the straw, as shown. Leave about 4 inches unwound.

4. Hold the straw with film behind the TV set. Slip each end of straw through a hole. Slip end of film through slit and pull until you can see a picture on the TV screen.

STRAW

5. Complete the TV set by pasting tabs in the order marked, to make a box.

6. Paste the end of film strip 3 to the middle of the second straw. Turn the first straw clockwise to bring the film back to the starting position in the TV set.

7. To watch your TV news film, pull the outside straw slowly to the side and watch the film move by on the TV screen. Then rewind the film on the inside straw, and you'll be ready to start again!

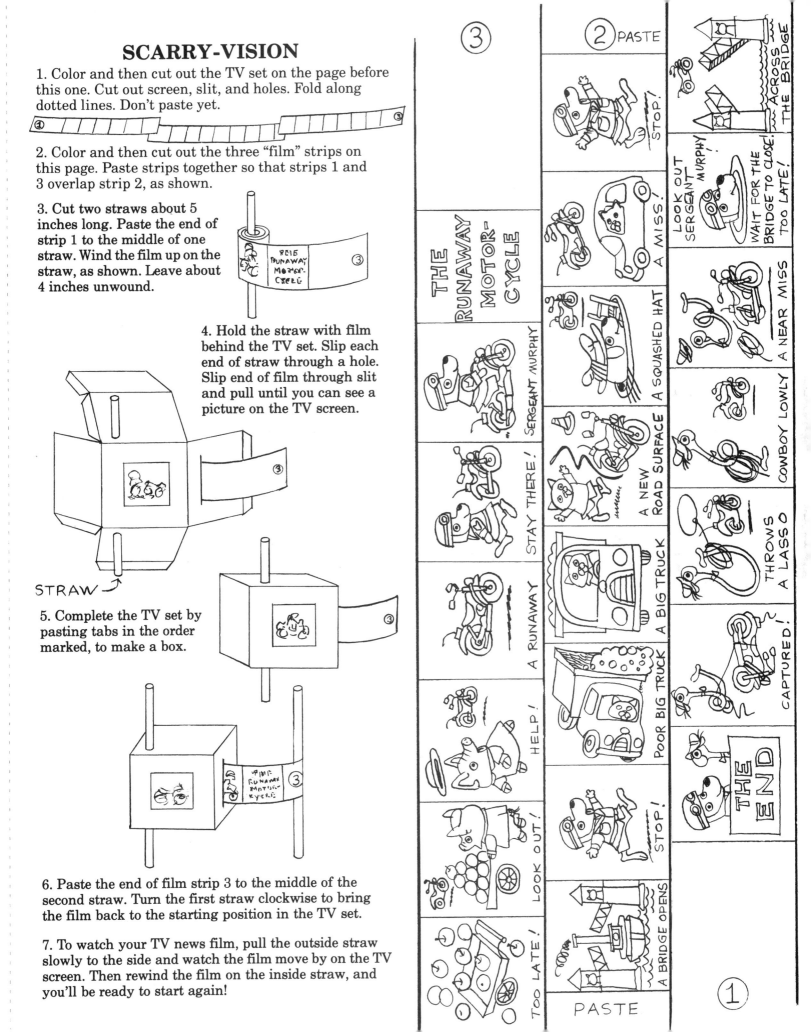

BUNNY HELICOPTERS

Color and cut out the bunnies. Cut between their ears, along the solid black line. Fold along the dotted lines. On each bunny, fold one ear forward and one ear back. Tuck tab inside and paste or tape in place.

Drop the bunny helicopters from up high and watch them spin to the ground.

WHIRRRRRHHHH!

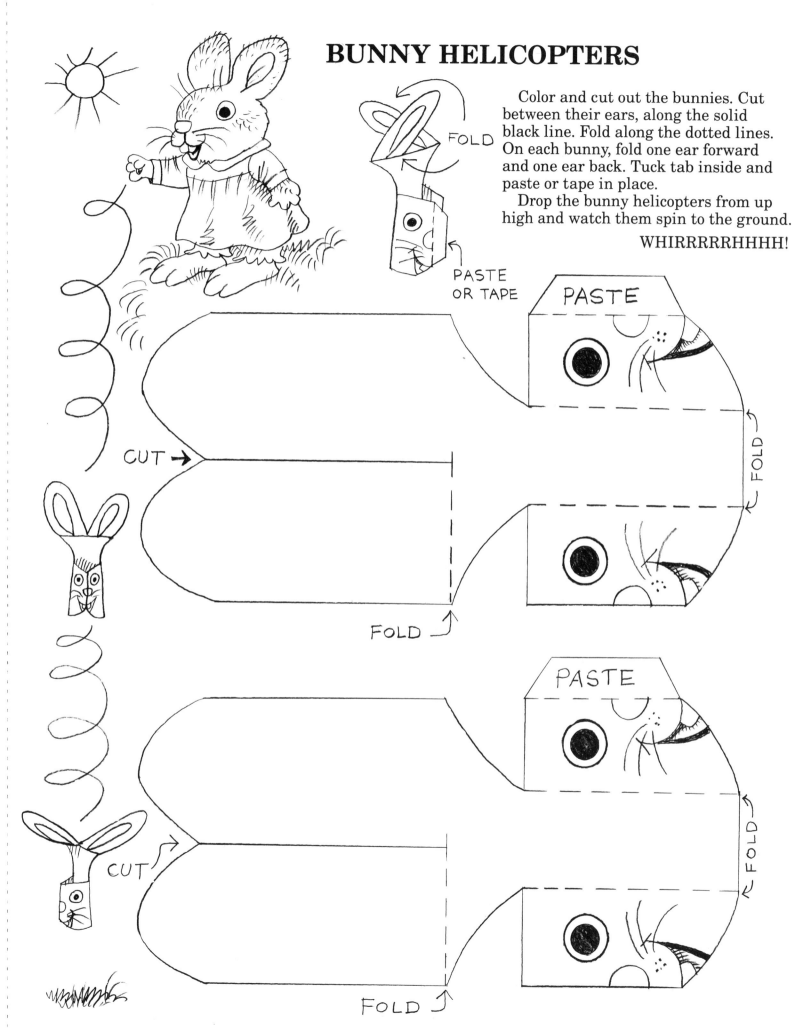

FOLD

PASTE OR TAPE

PASTE

CUT →

FOLD

FOLD

PASTE

CUT

FOLD

FOLD

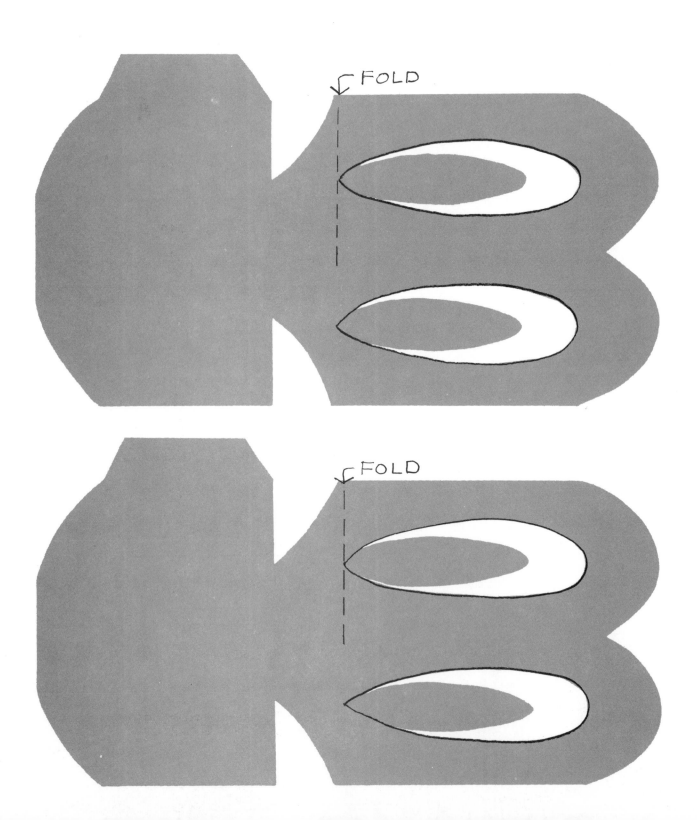

FOLD

FOLD

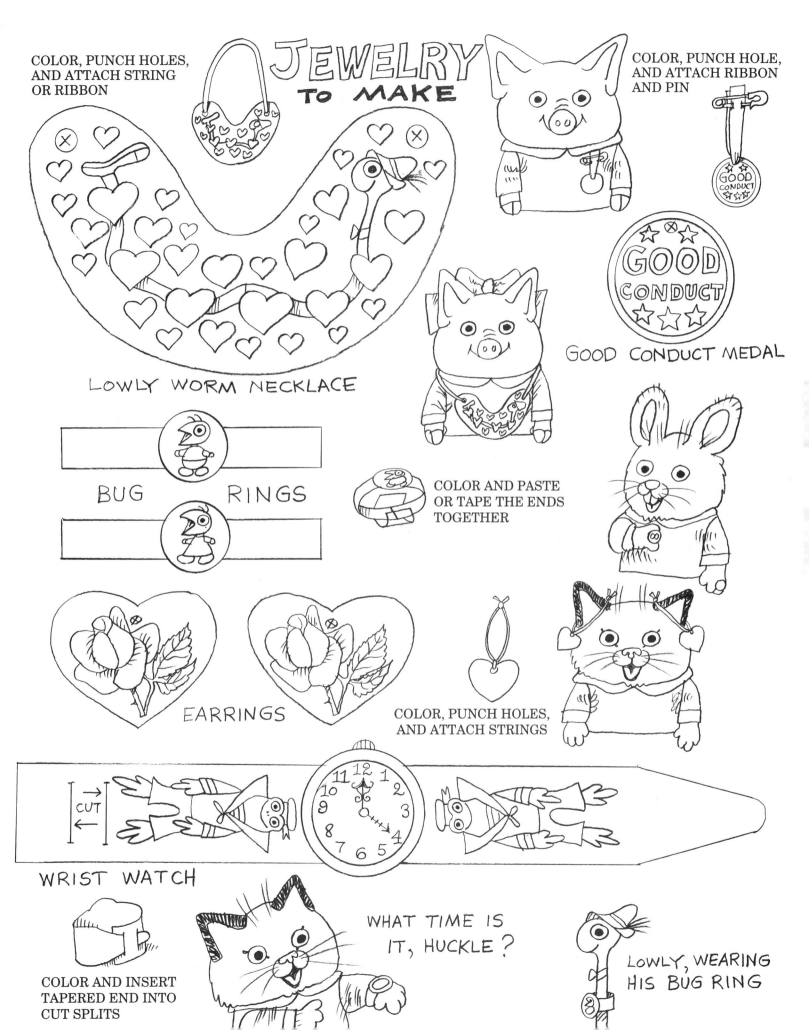

COLOR, PUNCH HOLES, AND ATTACH STRING OR RIBBON

JEWELRY TO MAKE

COLOR, PUNCH HOLE, AND ATTACH RIBBON AND PIN

GOOD CONDUCT

LOWLY WORM NECKLACE

GOOD CONDUCT MEDAL

BUG RINGS

COLOR AND PASTE OR TAPE THE ENDS TOGETHER

EARRINGS

COLOR, PUNCH HOLES, AND ATTACH STRINGS

WRIST WATCH

COLOR AND INSERT TAPERED END INTO CUT SPLITS

WHAT TIME IS IT, HUCKLE?

LOWLY, WEARING HIS BUG RING